Once upon a time there lived the Marriage Makers—three fairy godmothers. Their job was to find true love for all the triplets in their domain, including the Knight triplets. One by one, each fairy sprinkled her magic fairy dust…

And baby Anastasia got an overdose of intelligence and attitude! The last thing she needed was any man telling her what to do. Anastasia became *Too Smart for Marriage*.

"Cathie's writing always glows with warmth and charm."
—Jayne Ann Krentz

"Cathie is a great storyteller."
—Lass Small

"Love and laughter is never more delightful than from the clever pen of Cathie Linz."
—Melinda Helfer

Dear Reader,

We have two delightful, funny and charming LOVE & LAUGHTER stories for you this month! Cathie Linz concludes her MARRIAGE MAKERS miniseries with #51 *Too Smart for Marriage,* the story of the last remaining single Knight triplet, Anastasia Knight. She was blessed by her fairy godmother with a dash too much attitude and a heck of a lot of smarts, resulting in a woman who believes she has no use for marriage. Boy, is she about to be proved wrong!

Then bright new talent Bonnie Tucker continues her winning and hilarious storytelling in #52 *Stay Tuned: Wedding at 11:00.* It brings to mind the great classic romantic comedies like *His Girl Friday,* with lots of nineties spice! Don't miss the live, on-air wedding…maybe!

So take some time out of your busy schedule and enjoy the lighter side of love. Remember LOVE & LAUGHTER is 100% fat free!

Enjoy!

Malle Vallik

Malle Vallik
Associate Senior Editor

TOO SMART FOR MARRIAGE
Cathie Linz

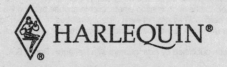

HARLEQUIN®

TORONTO • NEW YORK • LONDON
AMSTERDAM • PARIS • SYDNEY • HAMBURG
STOCKHOLM • ATHENS • TOKYO • MILAN • MADRID
PRAGUE • WARSAW • BUDAPEST • AUCKLAND

ISBN 0-373-44051-0

TOO SMART FOR MARRIAGE

Copyright © 1998 by Cathie L. Baumgardner

Printed in U.S.A.

Dear Reader,

Okay, I confess. I chose the ice-cream-parlor setting for this book because I'm a sucker for an old-fashioned banana split. Who wouldn't love owning their own ice cream parlor? And imagine the fun I had with research—every calorie was work related! My favorite homemade ice cream creation has hot fudge and caramel sauce poured over fresh pecans and soft vanilla ice cream.

The origins of ice cream are shrouded in myth, with credit going either to the Chinese, Nero (Claudius Caesar) in ancient Rome, or the chef of King Charles I of England. I've heard it on good authority that fairy godmothers actually created ice cream...once upon a time, give or take a few years.

I've had fun working on this special trilogy with Betty, Muriel and Hattie Goodie. This is the final book in my MARRIAGE MAKERS trilogy. I hope you enjoy reading Anastasia and David's story as much as I did writing it! And if you should feel a craving for ice cream, try this fast and easy recipe for Mud Pie!

Happy reading...and eating!

Cathie Linz

MUD PIE
1 quart coffee ice cream, softened
1 prepared chocolate cookie pie crust (9 inches)
1/2 cup chocolate syrup

Spread ice cream into crust, pour chocolate syrup on top and swirl with a knife. Cover and freeze for at least two hours. Serve frozen.

Special thanks to:

Bill Phillips
for his talent for naming places,
to Susan Elizabeth Phillips
for a million things, including
title brainstorming
and to
Sharon Lawrence at Downers Grove Public Library
for introducing me to THE FROG PRINCESS.
Reddit! < grin >

Prologue

"I JUST LOVE WEDDINGS," Hattie Goodie said, her gossamer wings quivering.

"I must say, they've put out a good spread." Betty, the oldest Goodie triplet, nodded in approval as she viewed the tables laden with delectable goodies from lobster hors d'oeuvres and cold shrimp to chocolate-covered strawberries and white chocolate fondue. Her blunt-cut Prince Valiant hairdo matched her equally blunt personality.

"It's a good thing that, as fairy godmothers, we don't have to worry about calories." This comment came from the third sister, Muriel, in her down-to-earth way. She was sitting on top of the pile of gifts displayed on a side table in the ballroom. Hattie, who loved being higher than anyone else, perched on the biggest present while Betty marched along the table edge like a general at a battle site.

"I can't believe you two would dress so casually for such an elegant occasion." Hattie, fully decked out in a lavender gown and wide-brimmed picture hat with shoes and purse dyed to match, sniffed her disapproval of her sisters' attire. "Betty, a T-shirt is simply not appropriate at a *wedding* reception."

"I didn't want to outshine the bride," Betty retorted, smoothing out the wrinkles from one of her favorite T-shirts. "Read it and weep." She pointed to the wording: Fairy Godmothers Fly Because They Take Themselves Lightly. "Besides, we're invisible, for petunia's sake."

"One must still keep up appearances," Hattie stated primly.

Betty snorted with unladylike and unfairy-godmotherlike loudness.

Sensing she wouldn't win this particular battle, Hattie redirected her ire toward Muriel. "And you, wearing that khaki photographer's vest. It's not like you even *own* a camera."

Muriel just shrugged. "I like all the pockets."

Recalling the fight she'd had with Muriel a few weeks before when she'd tried to give her sister a makeover, Hattie decided to let sleeping dogs lie— or, in this case, let fashion-challenged fairy godmothers remain hopelessly out-of-date. Instead she focused her attention on their surroundings once more. "At least the ballroom is beautifully decorated, even if you two aren't," she couldn't help adding.

The Carousel Banquet Hall was awash in white tablecloths and lavender napkins. White fairy lights glittered, revealing flowers and more flowers. In the far corner of the ballroom, dressed in an elegant confection of satin and antique lace, the bride was feeding a generous slice of wedding cake to her groom.

"I'm so pleased that Jason and Heather are *finally* married." Hattie dabbed her eyes with an embroidered lawn handkerchief. "I feared this day would never come."

"Ryan and Courtney did the sensible thing and eloped." Muriel's voice reflected her approval of her charges' actions.

This attitude came as no surprise to Hattie. Being a no-nonsense fairy godmother herself, Muriel approved of similar traits in humans.

"Jason thought Ryan was joking when he announced that he'd been transferred back to Chicago and was returning a married man," Betty said.

"Jason was just peeved that he wasn't the first of the Knight triplets to tie the knot," Muriel replied.

"He doesn't look peeved any longer," Betty noted. "He looks happy."

Muriel nodded. "So does Ryan."

"Which leaves us with their sister, Anastasia."

All three fairy godmothers directed their attention toward the dark-haired young woman in a sleek lavender bridesmaid's dress. Her long hair was coiled on top of her head, displaying a pair of dangling earrings that upon closer examination turned out to be miniature books. She'd exchanged her strappy dress heels for a pair of comfortable white running shoes.

"Okay," Betty stated. "This time we're going to take a different approach to our work. With Jason and Ryan we were sort of flying by the seat of our pants—"

"No *sort of* about it," Muriel interjected. "We were *definitely* flying by the seat of our pants."

Betty frowned. She hated being interrupted. "Ever since we began this job of fairy godmothering and then inadvertently spilled too much fairy dust on our little charges at their christening, we've been dealing with our mistake while trying to unite them with their soul mates. Since then, we've dealt with a number of other triplets born in our jurisdiction with a fair amount of success. But the Knight triplets have always been unique.''

"Probably because we gave Jason too much sex appeal and common sense as a baby, while his brother Ryan got too much stubbornness and humor.''

"Don't forget Anastasia. Too much intelligence and attitude. It looks good on her, though, don't you think?'' Hattie said proudly.

"Anything would look good on her,'' Muriel admitted.

Turning their attention back to the wedding, the sisters saw that the guests had started dancing. The music, provided by the state-of-the-art sound system supplied by Heather's employer, radio station WMAX, filled the large ballroom. The song was "The One'' by Elton John, which had a special place in Jason and Heather's hearts. The newlyweds looked blissfully happy, as did Ryan and Courtney.

Anastasia, however, did not appear to be equally pleased. She was dancing with a stocky man who was more than a bit tipsy. When the guy made the mistake of groping Anastasia's bottom, she stomped on his foot.

"Too much attitude,'' Betty stated with a shake of her head.

Hattie immediately leaped to her charge's defense. "She was more than provoked. That lounge lizard had no business acting in such an ungentlemanly manner!'' With a look of undisguised disdain, she straightened her hat, her white-gloved fingers checking the purple bow fastened beneath her chin.

"She's going to be a handful," Muriel said. "Do we know who her soul mate is yet?"

"Of course we know. It's our job to know," Betty stated.

"David Sullivan. A tough cookie who doesn't believe in dreams," Hattie admitted.

"Which is one of the reasons I think we need to have a specific plan for Anastasia," Betty continued.

"We always say we have a plan, but it rarely works," Hattie said.

Betty shifted uncomfortably. "Yes, well, I'll admit that sometimes accidents do happen—"

"They sure do, and have you noticed that they seem to happen to us more often than to most?" This observation came from Muriel.

"Which is why we're going to call in some backup," Betty said.

"A guardian angel?" Hattie said the words reverently.

"No, a grandmother."

"A grandmother?"

"That's right. We need a human assistant in our matchmaking endeavors. One who can keep an eye on things," Betty said. "After all, we *do* have other charges to keep track of."

"What's with all this *we* stuff?" Muriel asked. "I thought this was Hattie's assignment and we're only here to advise. That's what you told me when my assignment was to make Ryan fall in love. I mean, Hattie is the one who spilled too much attitude and intelligence on baby Anastasia."

"Come on now," Betty said. "You know our motto. All for one and one for all."

"That's the Three Musketeers."

"Well, if it's good enough for them, it's good enough for us. Now, where was I?"

Hattie replied, "You said you were going to get human assistance on this case. A grandmother."

"Right." Betty nodded. "I've enlisted David Sullivan's grandmother to our cause."

"Is that allowed?" Hattie sounded uncertain.

Betty shrugged. "I won't tell, if you don't."

"Why can't David and Anastasia just meet and fall in love at first sight?" Hattie asked wistfully.

Betty shook her head. "That would be too easy."

"What's wrong with easy? Easy is good," Muriel said.

"It may be good, but it's not our lot in life. Come on," Betty coaxed in her hearty voice. "Where's your sense of adventure? Any trio of fairy godmothers could handle easy cases. It takes specialists like us to come up with innovative ways to deal with the really challenging ones."

"What is it that we're specialists in exactly?" Hattie inquired uncertainly.

"Trouble." Muriel's answer was succinct.

"Creating it or fixing it?" Hattie asked.

"Both, I'm afraid. But that's about to change. Claire Sullivan wants to see her only grandson settled down. She's raised him since his parents died when he was ten. David listens to his grandmother. With her on our side, this will be a piece of cake.''

No sooner were Betty's words spoken than there was a scuffle over by the wedding cake. Anastasia was angrily shrugging off the unwanted attention of her stocky dance partner, who still hadn't gotten the message despite the earlier stomping she'd given his foot. She shoved him. In his tipsy state, he stumbled backward, his arms windmilling as he froze for a moment before falling smack-dab into the middle of the wedding cake.

"A piece of cake," Muriel noted mockingly. "Yeah, right."

1

"DENTON WOULDN'T keep his mitts off me. I only gave him a small shove, but since he was already drunk, he lost his balance and ended up flattening my brother's wedding cake. And that's how I ended up ruining Jason's reception last weekend," Anastasia Knight told her friend, Claire Sullivan, as the two of them headed north on Chicago's Lake Shore Drive.

Anastasia was driving her vintage red Triumph convertible, her dark hair gathered in a ponytail to prevent it from whipping in the wind. The August day was warm but a cool breeze off the lake kept the temperature reasonable.

Claire had tugged a Chicago Cubs baseball cap low on her head to keep her hairdo in place. For someone in her seventies, Claire looked younger than her years, especially in the sapphire jogging suit she was wearing.

"Oh, dear." Claire shot her a concerned look. "Was he very angry?"

"Who?" Anastasia asked as she adeptly scooted the car around slower traffic. She drove the way she lived—with confidence and a dash of excitement. "Denton? Or Jason?"

"Denton deserved what he got," Claire stated. "I meant Jason."

"He wasn't real pleased, but Heather was a brick. She got everyone laughing and then distracted the crowd by gathering us together so she could throw her bouquet."

"And how did that go?"

"Well, Heather's maid of honor was her radio-show producer, Nita Weiskopf. She sure isn't the shy sort. Nita was right in front—ready to do whatever it took to grab that bouquet. I was way in the back."

"Being the shy sort yourself," Claire noted with a teasing grin.

"Yeah, right." Anastasia grinned back. "We both know I don't have a shy bone in my body. I was in the back because I didn't want to catch that bouquet and get stuck being the next bride."

"You've got something against brides?"

"Not at all. As long as I'm not one of them. I like my freedom too much. Anyway, Heather threw the bouquet straight toward Nita. Then the strangest thing happened." She paused for a moment. "Despite my best efforts to stay away from the blasted thing, it suddenly veered, and landed right on top of me. It was either catch the flowers or get hit in the head by them."

"How lucky for you!"

"I wouldn't call that lucky. Meeting you at the library, now *that* was lucky." Anastasia had felt an immediate affinity with the older woman, and their friendship had continued to grow over the past year.

"It was a red-letter day for me, as well," Claire

fondly declared. "As is today. Think of it. Me, a businesswoman. I can still scarcely believe it."

"You'll be great."

"I've wanted to open my own ice-cream parlor for years, but it was always just a dream, one I never thought I'd be able to see fulfilled."

"It was a stroke of luck that the owners of the building where I live decided to sell now," Anastasia said. "The store on the main floor has that wonderful marble counter, perfect for your ice-cream parlor. The place was just crying out to be renovated. I can't believe that, after the Polish deli located there closed, the storefront stood empty for a year." Pausing to give Claire a grin, she added, "You know you've got a good tenant in me. And when you rent out the third-floor apartment, you'll have another regular income."

"I know. I can't wait to get started with the renovation on the storefront. I hope to open up for business in six weeks."

Fifteen minutes later, Anastasia parked on the street in front of her building. She'd barely turned off the car engine when Claire hopped out and hurried to the front door.

"Goodness, I'm so nervous I can't even undo the lock." The older woman paused to squeeze Anastasia's hand. "Thanks again for coming with me to the real-estate closing. It meant a lot to me that you were there to hold my hand."

Anastasia hugged Claire. "That's what friends are for."

"I was hoping my grandson would be back from

his conference in New York to come with me...but I guess he got tied up.''

Anastasia wanted to tie *him* up and talk some sense into the bum. There was no love lost between Anastasia and Claire's grandson, David. Not that she'd ever actually met the guy, but that didn't stop her from disliking him. He sounded like a workaholic who didn't take the time to really appreciate his grandmother, who was a pretty incredible woman.

Claire's sky-blue eyes were clear and bright, and her auburn hair showed no sign of white, thanks to her religious visits to Paula's PowderPuff Beauty Salon, which she'd confessed she'd been going to since Eisenhower was president. And Claire had a big heart. She deserved better than a grandson who wasn't there when she needed him.

"Forget about David. Here..." Anastasia unlocked the door, opening it with a flourish. "Welcome to... Have you decided what to name your ice-cream parlor yet?"

"Not yet." Claire rushed inside. Standing in the middle of the snowflake-patterned terrazzo floor, she twirled and shouted, "Mine! All mine!"

Anastasia laughed at her friend's exuberance. Like Claire, she could see the possibilities here even though the vacant storefront wasn't looking its best at the moment. The previous owner of the building had passed away last year and his heirs had argued amongst themselves before finally deciding to sell the property.

They hadn't bothered fixing up the storefront, but the two apartments above were in good shape. The three-story red-brick building, built in the 1920s, was located in the northern suburb of Evanston, a hop, skip and jump from Chicago's city limits. Situated on a corner, it got enough passing traffic to bring in customers, without too much congestion to make it difficult to park. The storefront was also close enough to Northwestern University's campus for students to frequent it as well.

All in all, it was the perfect place to make dreams come true. And Anastasia was determined to do whatever she could to make Claire's dreams come true.

"What the hell is going on here?" The furious question came from a glowering but gorgeous guy standing inside the front door they'd both forgotten to lock. He looked mad enough to do serious damage to someone.

"Back off!" Anastasia's voice was powerful and curt, just as her self-defense teacher had taught in his class. Ever the city dweller, she reached into her oversize purse for a can of pepper spray. Keeping her eyes fixed on the man's face, she aimed it in his direction. Better to be safe than sorry. "Stay away!"

Far from being intimidated, the intruder had the gall to give her a mocking look. "Or what?" he drawled. "You'll suffocate me with shaving cream?"

Looking down, she realized she'd grabbed the can of lady's shaving cream she'd picked up at the drugstore earlier that day.

"David, what a surprise!" Claire exclaimed, coming closer to give him a big hug. "I thought you were still at that conference in Buffalo."

"I just got in and heard your garbled message on

my answering machine. It sounded as if you said something about buying an ice-cream parlor..."

"I left this address, but I didn't think you'd drive all the way over here to see the place yourself. And as soon as you got home, too. What a dear boy you are."

Boy? Anastasia thought in disbelief. There was nothing boyish about this man. He had Black Irish good looks, with dark hair and eyebrows. His wonderfully thick lashes framed incredibly blue eyes. Although it was only three in the afternoon, his angular jaw was shadowy with a hint of stubble. He looked tired and a little disreputable, as if he'd had a rough trip.

He was dressed in jeans that had seen their fair share of wear and a denim shirt that molded his broad shoulders. The rolled-up sleeves displayed his tanned arms. He was well-built, more on the lean-and-mean side than the pump-iron muscular side. She guessed him to be about six-two.

"What's going on here?" David demanded again.

"This—" Claire gave a sweeping motion around the dusty storefront "—is my future."

"No, it's not," David immediately corrected her. "Your nest egg in the bank is your future."

"Not any longer. I traded it in on this."

David paled beneath his tan. "You did *what?*"

"You don't have to shout, dear." She shot him a mildly reprimanding look. "I may be in my seventies, but I'm not deaf yet."

"I can't believe you'd do something like this without consulting me first," he said disapprovingly.

"You've been so busy lately, I haven't wanted to bother you."

Was that a flash of discomfiture Anastasia saw on his face or was it just a trick of the lighting? She couldn't be sure because now his expression was one of total anger. "You shouldn't have done this. Tell me, what *exactly* have you done?"

"Bought this building." Claire patted a wall fondly.

David looked as if his grandmother had hit him with a two-by-four. "Bought it," he carefully repeated. "As in paid money for it?"

"That's right. And got a mortgage on it," Claire added.

"What on earth possessed you to do that?"

"I'm going to open an ice-cream parlor. I told you on your answering machine."

"An ice-cream parlor. Did some fast-talking franchiser get hold of you and con you out of your money?"

"Of course not. My ice-cream parlor will be a throwback to earlier times, when the ice cream was homemade," she said proudly.

"Don't you think it's a little late in life to be starting a project like this?" he said. "Running a business these days is more trouble than it's worth. You should be spending your retirement years enjoying yourself, not tied down to working here all hours." David spoke to his grandmother as if he was admonishing a stubborn child, infuriating Anastasia on Claire's behalf.

The big galoot had his nerve! Anastasia was too

angry to speak. Luckily Claire was calm and eager to convince David of the wisdom of her action. Personally, Anastasia thought it was a waste of time. The guy clearly had a closed mind. Closed, hah! It was locked up tighter than Fort Knox.

"The two apartments upstairs are in good shape," Claire was telling him, "but the storefront does need a little work."

"A *little* work?" David repeated, looking around in disbelief. "It needs a miracle!"

"I thought that maybe you could help us fix it up." Claire gazed at him expectantly. "You're starting your leave of absence now, right?"

"Right, but..."

"I plan on having my grand opening in six weeks, on October first," Claire said with excitement.

David's voice dripped with gloom. "Even I know that's long past the high-demand period for ice cream."

"Ice cream is *always* in demand," Anastasia said finally. "Besides, properties like this in such a good location are rare and Claire couldn't just wait around until next summer."

David focused his angry gaze on Anastasia. "And you are...?"

"Oh, please excuse my poor manners," Claire exclaimed, pressing her hands to her flushed cheeks before fluttering them in his direction. "David, this is Anastasia Knight, a friend of mine. You remember, I told you about her."

"No, you didn't. Just like you didn't tell me about this place."

"I most certainly did tell you about Anastasia. I don't have all that many friends."

"The only friend you told me about is that mousy children's librarian."

Claire frowned. "Mousy?"

David shrugged. "I forget exactly how you described her, but all librarians are the same. I think it's great that you found some old woman to hang out with." He paused, belatedly aware of the hostility in the room. Maybe he wasn't the most silver-tongued guy on the block, but then tact wasn't exactly his strong suit. And he'd had a hell of a trip from Buffalo. He attempted to regain lost ground. "I meant it's great you found an older woman to, uh, befriend you."

His normally sweet-tempered grandmother was shaking her head in irritated disapproval. What, now his grandmother was going to object to him calling her old? Then what was the politically correct term? "A preretirement woman to be your buddy?" he tried hopefully.

The two glares he received in return let him know he wasn't even in the ballpark. And the impatient tapping of Anastasia's orange gym shoes gave him the impression that she was particularly offended by his comments.

"I never said my friend was old, older or preretirement age," Claire firmly stated. "Nor did the adjective *mousy* ever come into the conversation."

David was getting a bad feeling about this.

"Let me guess," he said.

"I'm the mousy old librarian," Anastasia confirmed for him.

2

SHE SURE DIDN'T LOOK like any librarian David had ever seen. Not that he spent much of his time hanging out in libraries. He'd never had the time or the inclination.

His job as an arson investigator had consumed his life for the past few years. Investigating fires that had often resulted in families losing their dreams or even their lives was enough to turn even a starry-eyed optimist into a cynic, and David had never been starry-eyed or an optimist. Not since his parents had been killed in a car crash when he'd been a kid.

His parents had been dreamers. His dad cashed in his life insurance policy on a get-rich-quick scheme, leaving nothing but debts. He knew that his grandparents had faced many financial and emotional hardships, although they never said or hinted that he was a burden to them.

Ever since David had been a kid, he'd been hardworking and practical, scoffing at the other kids' grandiose dreams of being a basketball star or rock singer. When he'd heard a fire chief give a speech at his school's career day presentation, he'd known that he'd found his line of work. After college he'd started out as a firefighter and then moved up in the ranks until he was transferred to the arson investigation division.

His cynical outlook had increased with every year he'd worked. What was the point of even having dreams when they could go up in a puff of smoke? When they could blind you to the reality of life, the way they'd blinded his father, leaving him and his grandparents to pick up the charred pieces afterwards? Over the years too many bad things had happened to good people for David to believe in much of anything anymore.

He'd taken this leave of absence at his boss's request, to get a better perspective on things and to use the vacation time that had been piling up for the past eight years.

Problem was, the thought of doing nothing drove him up a wall. He wasn't the type to sit around contemplating his navel and pondering why the Cubs hadn't won a pennant in his lifetime.

So he'd planned on spending some time making sure his grandmother was set up for her retirement. She was his only family, and he felt badly that he hadn't spent much time with her lately, but he was here now and he wasn't about to let someone take advantage of her sweet disposition. His instincts told him that Anastasia was definitely a bad influence on his grandmother, a woman who hadn't changed banks or hairdressers in umpteen decades. Buying a rundown building with the crazy idea of opening an ice-cream shop was totally out of character for her.

But not for the wild woman who'd threatened him with a can of shaving cream. He had a feeling this sort of thing was just in a day's work for her. He suspected she'd played a major role in his grandmother's totally uncharacteristic act of blowing her retirement nest egg. As his grandmother herself had admitted a few minutes ago, she didn't have that many friends, so there weren't many people who would have that kind of influence over her.

He gave the librarian another look, a male-to-female one this time. She wore confidence like a championship ring. Only a confident woman would get away with an outfit like the one she had on. The yellow sleeveless dress was long enough to brush the tops of her orange gym shoes, but she made it look sexy. For some reason, the dress made him think of sultry summer nights, cool lemonade and stolen kisses.

Her long brown hair was gathered up into a ponytail, accentuating her unusual golden eyes. She was tall, probably five-eight, which meant the top of her head came to just beneath his chin. Not that he saw himself getting that close to her. She had the attitude of a woman who was used to getting her own way. She was beautiful, but definitely not his type. And he didn't trust her.

David tried to keep blatant suspicion out of his voice as he said, "So, Anastasia, you're here as a buddy to help my grandmother fix up this place, is that it?"

"Actually, I live here. Well, not down here in the storefront, obviously," she added, her ponytail bouncing like a teenager's as she turned her head. "I meant that I live in one of the apartments upstairs."

"That's handy," he noted mockingly. So, his instincts had been on the mark. "And I suppose you were the one who recommended that my grandmother buy this..." He was going to say "broken-down dump," before deciding that might not be the best thing to do. "This old building."

Claire answered on Anastasia's behalf. "When Anastasia told me she'd found the perfect place for my ice-cream parlor, I couldn't believe it at first."

"I don't blame you," David murmured, deciding then and there he wouldn't believe anything Anastasia said without checking it out for himself first. The little con artist had probably talked his grandmother into buying this building in order to get her as a landlady, for one thing. How handy to have a landlady who was also a close friend, someone who wouldn't mind if you were a little late on your rent, or even if you didn't pay your rent at all. "What else have you been doing for my grandmother, Anastasia?"

"I went with her to the real-estate closing this morning."

David cursed silently. So the closing had only been a few hours ago. Dammit! If his originally scheduled flight hadn't been canceled because of bad weather, he would have gotten home early this morning and might have been able to stop his grandmother from this foolishness.

He had no doubt buying the building was a mistake. What kind of security was there in owning an ice-cream parlor? Let alone opening it in the fall. It didn't take a genius to figure out the idea was a stupid one.

"As I said before, Gran, owning a business might sound like a fun thing to do, but the reality is something else again. There are so many issues to deal with—hiring help, doing bookkeeping, taxes." He went on in detail for some time before ending with, "It really isn't a practical proposition."

"Sure it is. Anyone with the least bit of imagination could see that."

It came as no surprise that the heated words came not from his grandmother but from Anastasia. A shaft of golden sunlight was shining on her from the front window, creating a halo around the tousled strands of her long brown hair. But there was nothing angelic about her appearance. She looked passionate and exotic. She looked like the type of woman to disrupt a man's peace of mind and fill an old lady's head with foolish ideas.

"How did you meet my grandmother?" he asked Anastasia.

"We met at the library where I work, along with a bunch of other mousy old librarians," she added tartly.

David grimaced. So she wasn't about to let him off the hook. Fine by him. She wasn't exactly on the top of his hit parade at the moment, either.

"Your grandmother saved my neck," she said with a fond look at Claire.

Which he translated to mean that his grandmother had probably lent her money. He might not know much about librarians, but he'd heard that they didn't get paid much.

"Now, dear, don't tell him that story," Claire protested.

Bingo, David thought to himself. Something they didn't want him to know, which meant it was something he needed to find out. "Why not? I'd love to hear how you saved her neck, Gran."

"Well, it's a little embarrassing." Claire chuckled self-consciously. "You see, things are kind of tight at the library, what with the recent budget cuts and all. Anastasia often kiddingly says that being a librarian is like taking a vow of poverty."

Unless you find a rich elderly friend you can con into buying the ramshackle building where you live, David cynically thought. Maybe she was in cahoots with the previous owners. No doubt Anastasia, the little con artist, had even more self-serving schemes in mind for his grandmother.

"So I volunteered for the storytelling hour," Claire was saying. "That's where we first met."

"How did that save your neck?" David directed his question to Anastasia.

"Obviously you've never tried to read a story to twenty-five preschoolers," she replied.

David shuddered at the very idea. His experience with very young kids was very limited. He was more accustomed to working with them when they were older, old enough to hit a home run in the Little League baseball games he helped out with.

"I actually had two sets of twins in the group who were particularly rambunctious," Anastasia was saying, her smile a mixture of humor and horror. "They were running wild, making me wish I had ten more hands. I used to have an assistant to help out, but when she quit, her position wasn't filled. Attrition, they call it. I call it shortsighted stupidity, but hey, don't get me started on fiscal policy.''

"I won't.'' He doubted his views on monetary responsibility matched hers.

"Anyway, your grandmother, sweetie that she is, stepped in and prevented Terry the Terrible, one of the twins, from cutting my hair with a pair of scissors he'd somehow managed to confiscate. Claire is great with the kids. And she tells them the best stories.''

Claire was shaking her head as she smiled. "Not as good as Anastasia's stories. She makes up her own, you know.''

I'll bet she does, David thought.

"About a trio of fairy godmothers,'' Claire added. "She even does some drawings to go with her story. I've told her she should submit them, that they're good enough to be published.''

"So you really want to be a writer, Anastasia?''

"No. I'd really like to be independently wealthy so I could afford to be a writer,'' she said with an impertinent grin.

I'll bet you would. David was about to tell her that there was no way she'd get wealthy at his grandmother's expense, when Claire distracted him by grabbing his arm and tugging him to one side of the storefront. "David, take a look at this marble countertop—'' she ran her hand over it ''—and the snowflake-patterned terrazzo floor. Isn't it the cutest thing? This place really has tremendous potential. I was thinking that we need to open this room up, get rid of these extra strange little walls that chop the place up. I want to put the kitchen in the back."

"Kitchen?" he repeated. "What do you need a kitchen for?"

"To make the ice cream."

"Make it? I thought you were going to buy it."

Claire stared at him aghast. "Bite your tongue. Like I told you, my ice cream will be homemade. I'm even working on some special recipes. I found a soda-fountain book in with your grandfather's things. It has some old classic recipes."

"The Tune-In Sundae was one of my favorites," Anastasia said. "You decorate a block of ice cream to make it look like an old-fashioned radio. The Third Degree was also intriguing, but that was more of an ice-cream soda."

David wanted to give *her* the third degree and demand to know how she'd gotten herself so entwined in his grandmother's life while his back was turned. Anastasia had even apparently read his grandfather's soda-fountain book. David hadn't known his grandfather owned such a thing. His grandfather had died when David graduated from college, and while he knew his grandmother missed her husband terribly, David had never suspected that her loneliness would drive her to such foolishness.

Running one hand through his hair in frustration, he frowned at his grandmother. "Why didn't you talk to me before doing this?" he asked her once more.

Claire patted his hand. "I told you, dear...I didn't want to bother you when you were so busy. How was that conference you attended, by the way?"

"The conference was fine and I'm not too busy for something major like this."

"David is an arson investigator," Claire proudly informed Anastasia.

"So you've said." Unlike David, she remembered what Claire told her and the look she shot him informed him as much.

David ignored her. He wasn't about to get sidetracked. "Purchasing real estate is a big responsibility, let alone trying to start up a new business. Do you know how many businesses fail their first year? A majority of them," he answered for her. "And why an ice-cream parlor of all things?"

"Because your grandfather and I met in an ice-cream parlor where he was working as a soda jerk before the war. I'll never forget the first time I saw him." Her expression softened as her fingers caressed the smooth marble of the countertop. "He had such style and grace as he expertly tossed a scoop of ice cream over one shoulder to have it land in a metal banana-split dish. He had the best moves."

Looking over his shoulder, David noticed Anastasia's moves. Her sunshine-yellow dress clung to her hips with every step she took. She walked with a smooth sexy sway as she joined them.

"Everyone is entitled to a dream," Anastasia said, challenging him.

"Is that so?" David retorted as if speaking to a half-wit. "And what about responsible behavior and financial security?"

"Your grandmother put together a thorough financial plan to decide how much capital she'd need for her business. She's a smart woman. Can't you see she's doing something that makes her happy? Something that has deep personal meaning to her; bringing back memories of those early days with your grandfather. This is Claire's dream.''

David was stung by Anastasia's words and the implication that she knew his grandmother better than he did. ''And what kind of world would it be if we all went chasing after wild dreams?''

''A better one,'' Anastasia said tartly. ''Think about *that* while I go upstairs and change into some work clothes.''

''WELL, THAT WENT WELL,'' Hattie said as she hovered midair, her gossamer wings fluttering a mile a minute to keep her aloft. There wasn't a place in the storefront clean enough for her to perch on. With her free hand, she attempted to keep her electric-blue pillbox hat in place. It matched her dress right down to the pearl accents. Hattie prided herself on her ability to accessorize.

''Went well?'' Muriel repeated from the dusty marble countertop below. ''How can you say that?'' She shoved her fingers through her spiky white hair, which made her look like a disgruntled woodpecker, before stuffing her hands in the deep pockets of her khaki vest. ''Just because no blood was spilled?''

''You're such a fussbudget,'' Hattie retorted.

''Right,'' Muriel scoffed. ''This coming from the flibbertigibbet in the family.''

''Girls.'' Betty fixed them both with a reprimanding look as she began pacing along the countertop.

She was wearing her I Yell Because I Care T-shirt, which meant she wasn't in the mood to take any guff from anyone. "As I see it, we have a slight problem in that David thinks Anastasia is a con artist out to get his grandmother's money, not to mention that he doesn't believe in having dreams."

"I doubt he believes in fairy godmothers, either," Muriel interjected.

"It's early going yet," Betty said. "We just dropped by to check on the initial meeting and to make sure that Claire played her role as matchmaker. We don't have much experience putting ideas into the heads of strangers, but I must say that I'm pleased with the results."

"Are you sure that enlisting Claire's help is a good idea?" Hattie asked uncertainly.

Betty shrugged. "What can it hurt?"

"Only the entire balance of the universe, that's all," Muriel glumly replied.

"You must be brave," Anastasia said. "You must gather your courage. Remember your heritage."

The blue-eyed Himalayan cat she was speaking to just blinked at her from beneath the armchair it was cowering under.

"That mouse won't hurt you. I put a fresh piece of cheese in the humane live trap this morning. I'm sure he'll take the bait any moment and stop tormenting you. He's just running around to bother you. You really shouldn't let him get to you this way, Xena."

Anastasia had hoped that giving the feline a warrior princess's name would help her assertiveness problem, but so far no luck. She'd gotten the cat by default. Trevor, one of her former boyfriends, had given her the animal—dumped it on her, actually, saying he had no time for neurotic felines. Two days later, Anastasia had dumped Trevor but kept the cat.

"That mouse has no right bullying you," she said. "You need to assert yourself. Don't let him browbeat you, chase you under the chair this way."

The same could be true of David, she thought. He had no right trying to bully Claire in an attempt to send her scurrying under the proverbial chair.

Anastasia's view of him as a workaholic hardnose had been right on the money. The guy just didn't get it. He wouldn't know a dream from a hole in the ground.

Even so, she wasn't about to stand by and let him bully his grandmother into giving up her dream. It was his own fault that he hadn't been involved in Claire's decision. She'd no doubt guessed that he'd try to squash her dream instead of nurturing it the way Anastasia had. He was clearly a doubting Thomas.

She'd seen the suspicion in his eyes, incredible though they might be. Such an intense blue. It was a shame they were wasted on such an obstinate jerk.

So why did she feel this little curl of interest unfurling within her?

"Maybe that's lust, not interest," she muttered as she kicked off her shoes on her way to the bedroom. Once there, she tugged her dress over her head and replaced it with an orange sleeveless blouse and a pair of painter's white overalls. She liked her clothes colorful. She liked her surroundings the same way, and the brilliant blue and bright yellow color scheme in her bedroom certainly qualified.

There wasn't one item in the room that was neutral or white. The walls were yellow, while the handwoven Indian rug on the floor was blue with golden stars and moons. Additional splashes of color were evident in the Tiffany-style lamp on the dresser and the framed Van Gogh poster on the wall.

As she tugged the shoulder straps of her overalls into place, she replayed David's questions in her mind. He clearly didn't like her and he was suspicious. His type usually was. They didn't believe in random acts of kindness. If the car ahead of him on the Northwest Tollway paid his toll for him, he'd probably have it followed and investigated to find out what ulterior motive the driver had.

What had made him that way? Working as an arson investigator? Or losing his parents when he was young?

Why did she care?

It was those damn intense blue eyes. If only they'd been blah brown. And if only they hadn't been teamed with those Black Irish good looks. She'd always been a sucker for them, ever since "Remington Steele" had first aired on TV.

The guys in her life had usually shared Remington's devil-may-care attitude. They'd had big dreams, whether they'd come true or not. And okay, so they'd been somewhat immature and irresponsible, but that had been part of their charm. In the beginning.

Growing up with two bossy brothers, as the only

girl in a set of triplets, had ensured that she hadn't been attracted to the controlling intense type. David's type.

Maybe he wouldn't be around much. Maybe Claire was talking some sense into him at this very moment.

"I'M SO GLAD you agreed to help me fix up the place." Claire glowed at David. "I don't know anything about load-bearing walls and not being able to tear those down. You're so clever, dear. But then, you did work on construction sites all those summers while you were in college."

"That was years ago," David reminded her.

"I'm sure it's like riding a bike, something you don't forget. And you are on leave now, right, dear? Six weeks, I believe you said."

David nodded.

"Then it would be perfect timing. We could get a lot accomplished in the next six weeks."

Not the least of which would be David's finding out exactly what Anastasia was up to.

"And what about your building going condo?" Claire added. "Didn't you tell me that you'd have to move soon? Have you had time to find another place yet? Because if not, the apartment on the third floor is vacant and you'd be welcome to stay here for as long as you like."

"I might take you up on that."

"Oh, I hope you do. It would be so nice to have you here. And I wouldn't worry about leaving the place at night, not with you to look after things."

"Yeah, defending the place with a can of shaving

cream isn't much of a crime deterrent,'' David noted mockingly.

"Oh, you mustn't mind Anastasia. She was just trying to help me.''

"I know what she was trying to do,'' David said. And he knew what he had to do to combat it. Move in and look out for his grandmother's interests.

"IS HE GONE?'' Anastasia asked as she entered the storefront to find Claire alone.

"For now. I'm sorry David called you mousy,'' Claire apologized.

"Hey, I've been called much worse. He'll soon discover how wrong he was. About a lot of things.''

Claire nodded. "I love him dearly, but he does tend to be a mite...''

"Bossy, judgmental, impossible?''

"I was going to say serious.''

"That would have been my next guess.'' Anastasia grinned.

"He just needs someone to teach him how to loosen up,'' Claire said wistfully. "Someone who could help him understand the appeal of having dreams. And I know just the woman for the job.''

There was no mistaking Claire's hopeful look in Anastasia's direction.

"Who, me? Oh no you don't.'' Anastasia shook her head so vehemently her ponytail slapped against her cheeks.

"You'd be the perfect person to teach David how to dream...and how to have some fun in life. I've never met anyone so full of a zest for life as you.''

"I've got that zest because I don't hang around with serious guys like David who suck all the fun out of life." Seeing Claire's crestfallen expression made her feel badly. "I'm sorry. I know he's your grandson and you love him, but…"

"You're probably right, dear." Now it was Anastasia's turn to be on the receiving end of Claire's hand-patting. "I doubt that even you could manage to turn David around. You're good, but not that good."

"Now wait a minute." Anastasia didn't take kindly to hearing that. "I most certainly am that good. I could make him see the light—"

"And that would make him so much better to have around," Claire interjected. "Do you really want him reprimanding us for the next few weeks while he's helping us fix up the place, or would you rather bring him around to our way of thinking?"

"Wait a second. What's this about him helping us?"

"David has agreed to do some of the renovation work to help me save on expenses. And he's moving into the vacant apartment on the third floor."

"So he's going to be underfoot for a while." Anastasia paused to review her options. "In that case, I suppose it would be in our best interest to convert him to our way of thinking. Besides, it's not like I don't have experience with his type. My brother Jason was bossy and overbearing. I've knocked most of it out of him, though. Figuratively speaking, of course. A majority of the time it did not require bodily blows. But your grandson is much more…" How could she put it? Earthy? Her brother was good-looking. Heck, he'd been named Chicago's Sexiest Bachelor earlier in the year. But David was more than just handsome. He exuded raw masculinity the way an oven generated heat.

"He's much more what, dear?"

"Much more of a challenge," she substituted. "Not that I'm not intrigued by a challenge, because I am." She imagined herself making the bossy David see the light, showing him the errors of his ways.

Claire had a point. It would make the next few weeks much easier if he was with them instead of against them. And the fastest way to do that was to show him the value of having dreams and having fun.

"Tell me," Anastasia asked. "What does David do to have fun?"

"He works."

She sighed. "That's what I was afraid of. Okay, Claire, you've got a deal. I'll try and whip David into shape for you."

CRASH! The noise woke Anastasia from a sound sleep. Sitting upright in bed, she turned on the lamp and shot a bleary-eyed gaze at her Wallace and Gromit alarm clock. The British cartoon characters usually made her smile, but all she noted now was that it was almost two in the morning. The crashing sound seemed to have come from directly outside her front door.

Deciding it was better to fear the noise you knew rather than the one you didn't, she slid out of bed and tiptoed from her bedroom across the living room to her front door, turning on another light as she went along. She put her nose to her door, and cautiously peered out the peephole.

All she could see was a denim-clad rear end—a masculine rear end, most definitely. And a rather nicely formed one at that.

Then she saw the rest of the man as he straightened and shot a wary look over his shoulder at her door. It was David.

For two days she'd been waiting for him to finish packing up his stuff and finally show his face, and his rather nice bottom, here. She'd begun to wonder if he hadn't decided to back out of his agreement with his grandmother.

But now he'd shown up with a bang, or rather a crash and several inventive curses.

Making the most of the moment, she opened her door and, putting one hand on her hip à la Mae West, drawled, "Welcome to the neighborhood, big boy."

3

SWEARING, David dropped the box of athletic equipment he'd just picked up, narrowly missing hitting his foot. Feeling like a klutz, he glared at Anastasia and growled, "What are you, the welcoming committee?"

"You could say that." She showed no sign of remorse at having startled him. "So what made you decide to sneak into the building in the middle of the night?"

"I'm not sneaking."

"Really?" One of her delicately curved eyebrows lifted in patent disbelief. "In that case, I stand corrected."

Actually, she was standing there in a modest white nightie that covered her from neck to ankle. But the light behind her showed off the outline of her figure through the thin cotton rather nicely. Never one to look a gift horse in the mouth, David paused to enjoy the view.

She had the kind of lush body made for a lingerie catalog. It seemed a crime to cover it up the way she did. Her long hair was tousled around her shoulders as if she'd just gotten up from a warm bed. She was an unusual mixture of cool class and brash attitude.

"You do realize what time it is, don't you?" Her voice was husky and sleepy, a sexy combination. A moment later she shifted, moving out of the revealing pool of light as she took a step closer to him to peer into the open box at his feet.

"Dumbbells," she murmured. "How...appropriate."

He frowned. "What's that crack supposed to mean?"

"Nothing. How much longer do you think you'll be making a racket in the hallway? I'm just wondering because I do have to get up at seven."

David was already up and he wasn't pleased with his body's traitorous reaction. He was here to keep an eye on Anastasia to protect his grandmother, not to ogle her like a teenager. Not that she hadn't done a bit of ogling herself. Those sly golden eyes of hers had slid over him like warm honey.

"I'm almost done here," he said, his voice raspy as he bent to pick up the box he'd dropped earlier.

"That's a relief. Well, have fun." With a yawn and a wave, she closed her door but paused long enough to add an irreverent grin. "You need any help, just whistle. You know how to whistle, don't you, David? Just put your lips together and blow."

As he watched the sexy sway of her hips as she sashayed back into her apartment, his mouth went dry, making it damn hard to whistle. Looking on the bright side, at least he wasn't drooling.

AT WORK the next day, Anastasia was prevented from thinking about David by the sheer number of things she had to get done. A group of kids from a local daycare center stopped by for a tour of the library, and then she was scheduled to work the reference desk for three hours, after which she had a staff meeting to attend.

The only break she got was to eat lunch, which she did in the staff room. She was about halfway through her cob salad when she got the message that there was a call for her. Picking up the extension, she was pleased to hear her mother's voice.

"I'm sorry to bother you at work, hon, but I tried to leave a message on your answering machine, only I couldn't get through because I kept getting a busy signal all morning."

"Xena must have knocked the phone off the hook in the bedroom," Anastasia replied. "I've been meaning to get a better phone, one that you can hang up properly instead of just setting down on a flat surface."

"While you're at it, maybe you could also get a better cat," her mom suggested. "One that would earn its keep by catching mice."

Sighing, Anastasia regretted ever confessing her mouse problem to her mother. "I don't want Xena eating mice. I don't want any mice deaths on my conscience."

"Your father could come over—"

"No, that's okay," she said quickly. She could imagine what her father would do. He had a way of overreacting and could end up flattening her apartment in his efforts to get the mouse. She was still recovering from the time he'd insisted on changing a ceiling-fixture lightbulb in the kitchen for her and ended up blowing all the fuses in the building. "I have the situation under control."

"Well, I'm calling to invite you to dinner this weekend. Mrs. Sanduski's son is in town and I thought you could meet him."

"Mom, no more fixing me up. You remember what happened the last time?"

"How could I know that Denton would get fresh at the wedding? He seemed like a nice young man. And he's been doing our taxes for three years now."

"Forget it." Anastasia's voice was firm. It was the only way to deal with her matchmaking mom. Sometimes she got this feeling that she was surrounded by matchmakers. "I've got a full social calendar on my own."

"Oh? You've met someone?" The question was filled with hopefulness.

Anastasia sidestepped it by saying, "I'm going to be very busy the next few weeks helping Claire get the storefront in order by October first."

"Why doesn't she hire someone?"

"She has, plus her grandson is helping her out…"

"And how old is he?"

"Thirty-something."

"Really?" Anastasia could practically see her mother's ears perking up. "And is he single?"

"I wish you wouldn't concern yourself with my love life."

"I just don't want you to be all alone, honey."

Anastasia shrugged. "Now you sound like Claire."

"Is she trying to fix you up with her grandson?"

"No." Or was she? Claire was the one who'd suggested that Anastasia teach David how to loosen up, how to have fun. And she'd invited David to move into the apartment upstairs, as well as having him supervise the renovations. Which meant that David would be underfoot all the time. He'd only moved in the day before, but already it felt as if the building was marked by his presence. "Listen, Mom, I've got to get back to work. Give Dad a hug from me, okay? And, remember, no more matchmaking!"

"HATTIE, DID YOU influence Anastasia's mom? Encourage her to meddle in Anastasia's love life?" Betty asked, fixing her sister with a reprimanding look, ignoring the many children around them in the library.

Hattie, perched nearby on a shelf, immediately began fiddling with her elaborately decorated straw hat, almost shredding it in the process. "No. Not really. Well, a little bit maybe. But not Denton. I had nothing to do with Denton grabbing her at the wedding. That was totally his idea. And a bad one at that."

"She's babbling," Muriel said. "A sure sign she's done something she shouldn't have."

"It was just a little something," Hattie replied. "I mean, you were the one, Betty, who said we needed to enlist human help. And I thought that if a grandmother was good, then a mother would be even better."

"Wrong," Betty said bluntly. "Anastasia is going to dig in her heels and get stubborn if she's got two people after her, trying to get her married off."

"It's not like I used much magic," Hattie protested. "I think her mother wants her to get married. I didn't have to do much convincing. You remember how bad Mrs. Knight was about Anastasia's dates when she was in high school? Asking all kinds of questions. Grilling them."

Betty nodded. "She made the Spanish Inquisition look like a good time."

"So I didn't really screw up here," Hattie continued. "Maybe my magic wand didn't even have an effect. That happens a lot, you know."

"Well, don't do it again," Betty ordered her. "No going off on your own and getting creative. Just stick to our game plan and we'll be fine. Limit your creative urges to your hats," she added as a bunch of grapes drooped from the overburdened straw brim. "That should keep you busy enough."

"Humans have a tendency to complicate matters," Muriel added.

"And we can do that just fine by ourselves," Hattie agreed.

ANASTASIA RETURNED from her busy day at the library to find Claire in the storefront, going through wallpaper books. Instead of using the separate front entrance from the street that led upstairs to her apartment, she paused to knock on the storefront's glass window.

Claire immediately bounced up to let her in. "You're just the person I needed to see," she exclaimed while dragging Anastasia toward a card table set up in the middle of the room.

"Why's that?" Anastasia asked.

"Wallpaper."

"Where's David?" She looked around. The only evidence of his presence was the large square of plywood resting on two sawhorses, the top of which was covered with various tools.

"He's stripping in the back," Claire said absently.

"Really?" Anastasia blinked at the image of David peeling the denim from his promising body before realizing Claire no doubt meant he was stripping wallpaper. "So..." She wiped her damp palms on her slacks. Was it her or was it suddenly *very* hot in here? "What can I help you with?"

"Wallpaper. I can't decide between this one—" Claire showed her a pink-and-white-striped sample "—or this one." She picked up another that featured ice-cream cones.

"I can't be objective about pink striped wallpaper," Anastasia ruefully confessed with a shake of her head. "Not since I was ten and drank chocolate milk while helping my dad put up the wallpaper in my bedroom."

Claire frowned in confusion. "I don't understand the connection."

"My brother Ryan told me a great knock-knock joke and I cracked up, spewing chocolate milk all over the pink stripes. It was a mess. Ever since then, I've been a firm believer that chocolate milk and pink wallpaper don't mix. And I also learned not to drink anything when my brother Ryan is in the vicinity."

"He's the one with the U.S. Marshal Service, isn't he?"

"That's right. He's recently been transferred back to this area after being in Oregon for several years. Typical of him, to surprise us all, he came back a married man. But then, I'd always liked Courtney, his new wife."

"So marriage is okay for your brothers, just not for you?"

"My brothers needed a smart woman to keep them in line," she airily informed Claire. Tucking her long hair behind her left ear, she added, "I don't need anyone keeping me in line, thank you very much."

"You wouldn't like to keep some man in line?"

Anastasia shrugged. "The guys I go out with tend to be on the laid-back end of the scale instead of being bossy. They don't need me to fine-tune them. But enough about me. What about a name for this place? Have you gotten any more ideas?"

"Let's see." Claire grabbed for her ever-present list. "So far we've got Super Scooper, but that sounds like something you'd use after taking a Great Dane for a walk."

"And then there's The Ice Cream Cometh," Anastasia added. That entry had been one of hers, a take on the play *The Iceman Cometh*. "But that might be too literary."

"I Scream, You Scream, but that sounds more like a horror shop." Claire shook her head.

"We'll just have to keep thinking. Listen, are we still on for that auction tonight?"

"You bet."

"What auction?" David asked as he joined them, wiping his hands on a rag. He wore dusty jeans and a white T-shirt, looking even more powerful and earthy than he had the previous two times she'd seen him. Why did sweat have to look good on him?

Still she kept her cool while replying, ''Your grandmother and I are going to an antique auction to get some furniture for the ice-cream parlor.''

''Not without me, you aren't,'' he said.

Instead of making a fuss, Anastasia just smiled at him and said, ''Fine by me.'' That should have been his first hint that something was up.

But no, like a sheep to slaughter, he'd blindly gone along, changing from his work clothes into dark slacks and a blue shirt. Heck, he'd even put on a tie, and now here he was, stuck on a folding chair, next to Anastasia and his grandmother, with a bunch of arts types looking at God-knows-what in the front of a crowded warehouse. To think he was missing a Cubs game for this.

''How much longer do we have to stay here?'' he leaned over to whisper in Anastasia's ear, inhaling the citrus smell of her perfume.

''Until the auction is over.''

He sighed. ''And how long will that be?''

Instead of answering she said, ''If you have someplace else you'd rather be, you're welcome to take a cab home.''

''And leave you and my grandmother here alone?'' He shot her a mocking look. ''I wouldn't dream of it.''

''No, you don't believe in dreams, do you? I wonder why that is,'' she mused.

''Because I'm practical. And I can tell you that no

practical person would pay this kind of money for stuff you can get at a garage sale.''

"It isn't *stuff*," she corrected him. "These are highly collectible pieces of art."

"Yeah, right," David scoffed. "Those dumpy couches, tables and lamps lining the outer walls are pieces of art?" He frowned at a particularly monstrous table with carved dragon legs.

"They most certainly are."

"And what about those glass showcases crammed full of junk?"

"There are some fine pieces of china and jewelry included in the display. Not junk."

"I guess there's a fool born every minute," he drawled.

"Apparently there is," she retorted sweetly, "since I'm sitting next to one right now."

"My grandmother is no fool," he said, deliberately misunderstanding her.

"No, she certainly isn't. But her bossy grandson shows all the signs of being one." She fixed him with a reprimanding look. "Maybe if you'd sit there with an open mind, you might learn something. Who knows, you might even enjoy yourself."

"I am enjoying myself," he murmured. He enjoyed watching the anger flash in her golden eyes, enjoyed watching her, period. The rest of the circus didn't hold much interest for him.

Up front, the auctioneer was launching into another spiel, sounding like a man on a caffeine overdose. "Two thousand, twenty-one, twenty-two hundred, I have twenty-two hundred. Who'll give me twenty-five?'' All this said in the space of five seconds. It was enough to make a sane person hyperventilate. The gavel banged and yet another worthless piece of junk was hauled off to some hapless bidder only to have the entire process start all over again.

The words blended into one another as David folded his arms against his chest and sat back in the half-dozing eyes-open state he used during staff meetings at work.

He hadn't gotten much sleep last night. He'd kept remembering Anastasia in that backlit nightie. The image had remained fixed in his mind no matter how much he'd tried to dislodge it.

Frowning, he lifted his hand to rub his nose.

The gavel banged. "Sold for eighty dollars to the man wearing the tie."

"Congratulations," Anastasia said with a grin he didn't trust. "You just outbid the others."

"What are you talking about? All I did was rub my nose."

"Dangerous thing to do at an auction."

"So what useless piece of junk did I get stuck with?"

"An erotic netsuke."

He choked. She pounded him on the back with eager vehemence.

Leaning away, David glared at her. He wasn't sure what a netsuke was, but he sure as hell knew the definition of erotic. "You made me bid on something X-rated. What the heck is netsuke, anyway?"

"It's a small Oriental carving. Highly collectible.

You've got a real keen eye for someone who thinks art is junk," she teased him.

He wasn't amused. This was all *her* fault. If he hadn't suspected that she'd try to lead Claire astray to bid on something outrageous at this stupid auction, he wouldn't have come along. But his grandmother had only bid on one thing, a wrought-iron table and two matching chairs the auctioneer had called an authentic bistro set. Instead, he was the one who'd bought something wild.

"Are you having fun yet?" Anastasia asked with an innocent bat of her long eyelashes.

"No," he growled.

"Then come out with me on Saturday for a picnic."

"Why?" he asked cautiously, still recalling the overexuberant pounding she'd given his back.

"So I can fit ya with a pair of cement boots and dump ya in the river," she growled like a 1920s gangster, before laughing. "Geez, talk about being suspicious. There's no risk involved. No strings. Just for fun. Unless you're not up to the challenge?"

"Fine. Saturday. A picnic." He hadn't been on one since he was ten, but how hard could it be? You grabbed some burgers and ate at a picnic table. Heck, his lunch hour at work might even qualify as a picnic...on those occasions when he ate a burger outside...in between exploring incinerated buildings to analyze burn patterns, among other things.

He could do this. And while he was at it, he might find out what Anastasia was *really* up to.

"Good," she said with a smile. "I'll bring the picnic. Meet you at my place at six."

He didn't dare nod for fear that doing so would leave him stuck with some other monstrosity on the auction block. "Fine."

"STEP ONE accomplished," Betty said from atop a glass case in the auction warehouse that was filled with pieces of Staffordshire china. "Things are moving right on schedule. I told you that drafting Claire's help would simplify matters for us."

"I can't believe that for once things are actually going according to plan," Hattie said from her perch atop a taller case filled with jewelry. "Did you see how cleverly Claire maneuvered Anastasia into agreeing to loosen David up the other day? And how deftly Anastasia just invited David out?"

"That doesn't mean he'll loosen up. He still doesn't trust her," Muriel said as she dusted off her photographer's vest before digging in the pocket for her favorite munchies—granola.

"Ignore Muriel." Betty impatiently shoved the bangs from her Prince Valiant haircut off her forehead and glared at her sister for rocking the boat. "Things will go smoothly this time."

"Maybe you should knock on wood when you say that," Hattie nervously suggested. "Just to be on the safe side."

"We're fairy godmothers. We're not supposed to

be suspicious," Muriel declared. "Look, it says so right here." She whipped out a thick rule book that was almost as big as she was and much fancier, complete with gilded pages and calligraphic printing. Using her magic wand, she zipped through the hundreds and hundreds of pages until she found the one she was looking for. "Rule number 1,359."

"We've already bent a few of the rules in that book," Hattie told her.

"Bent?" Betty scoffed as she zapped the book away. "For petunia's sake, we've *twisted* some of them so much they resemble pretzels."

"But is that a good thing?" Hattie anxiously asked.

"We're still here, aren't we?" Betty retorted.

"Well, yes." Hattie nodded and patted her silvery curls as if to verify that fact. "And while we're here, perhaps we should take a closer look at the Victorian hatpins in this glass case. I've always wanted one."

SATURDAY MORNINGS Anastasia liked sleeping in until ten. It was one of her few indulgences. But this morning, a horrible thumping noise woke her before dawn.

Squinting, she tried to focus on the digital readout on her Wallace and Gromit alarm clock. Five o'clock. She got déjà vu from the last time she'd been woken in the middle of the night. Judging from the fact that the incessant thudding was coming from directly above her, she suspected the culprit was the same— David.

Didn't the man ever sleep? What could he be doing up there? What if he wasn't doing it alone?

That made her pause in the midst of shoving the bedcovers off. Maybe she shouldn't just go upstairs and hammer on his door to tell him to be quiet. Unfortunately, she didn't have his phone number, otherwise she could call him.

Straightening the tangled strap on her peach-colored silk nightie, she reached for the phone and dialed information, only to be told that his number was unlisted. Probably to keep old neighbors from coming after him and harassing him for being so loud, she decided darkly.

Thud, *thump,* thud, *thump.* She tried putting her pillow over her head to muffle the noise. It didn't work. All she ended up doing was nearly suffocating herself. She needed more sleep. She couldn't maneuver on only four hours. It wasn't human. This was torture. He was doing it on purpose. Thud, *thump,* thud, *thump.*

Unable to take it any longer, she got out of bed to tug on a purple sweatshirt and matching pants sitting nearby. The outfit was grungy, but she didn't care. She wasn't going upstairs to seduce David, she was going to *silence* him. And read him the riot act. Because not only had David woken up Anastasia, he was distressing Xena, who didn't like loud noises. "Don't worry, kiddo." She lifted the blanket to assure the long-haired Himalayan who'd dived under the bedcovers. "I'll take care of this."

A few minutes later, she was on the third-floor

landing, in front of David's apartment. Her knock on his door went unanswered at first. So she pounded harder. Finally, she heard the locks being undone. A second later *she* nearly came undone as he stood there wearing nothing more than navy gym shorts and a guilty grin.

4

"DID I WAKE YOU UP?" he asked with a blink of his gorgeous blue eyes.

She refused to be impressed. "Whatever gave you that idea?" she drawled mockingly. "The fact that it's barely five in the morning?" *Barely* was the operative word here. His chest was bare, allowing her to see the well-formed muscles highlighted by a sheen of sweat.

He was leanly built, but solid. And he wasn't overly hairy. His legs were bare. Even his knees were great, not knobby like most guys she knew. But then most guys she knew weren't doing…whatever it was he'd been doing to wake her up in the first place. "You're making enough noise up here to wake the dead."

"I was exercising," he said.

"Alone?" she asked, not sure what constituted "exercising" in his book.

"Yes, alone." Grabbing a nearby towel, he absently wiped the sheen of sweat from his chest. "Why?"

"It sounded like there was a herd of elephants up here. What were you doing?"

"Jumping jacks."

Must be his fire department background, she decided. Only men in uniform did jumping jacks. Or, in David's case, men *out* of uniform. "Try tai chi instead," she suggested. "It's quieter."

"Tie who?" He frowned.

"Tai chi. An ancient Chinese form of exercise for the mind and body." At his blank look, she muttered, "Forget it. Remember this instead. I'm sleeping right beneath you."

Not the best way of putting it, she belatedly realized. The image her words had evoked was much more seductive than she would have liked. Hurriedly scanning his face and seeing the passionate intensity of his expression, she suspected he was sharing a similar vision—of her sleeping beneath him, their legs tangled, his weight resting against her like a sexy comforter.

She saw his blue eyes darken, making her very much aware that he was standing there half-naked while she was a mere two feet away still wearing her nightie under her sweatshirt and pants. She was acutely aware of the sensual silk rubbing against her skin as he looked at her as if he could see beneath her clothing, making her tingle from the inside out.

Startled, she took a quick step back, almost tripping on the overly long hem of her droopy sweatpants. Tugging up the waistband may not have been the classiest move, but it brought her back to reality as she lifted her chin in a don't-mess-with-me move. She just needed more sleep, that was her problem. "No more jumping around up here or I'll have to complain to our landlady."

"I've known my grandmother longer than you have," he said. "What do you think she'll do to me? Ground me?"

"No, I think she'll give you one of those reprimanding looks that lets you know you're in the doghouse without her saying a word."

To her surprise he actually grinned. He didn't look half-bad when he did that. Okay, so he looked pretty damn good. Not that she was impressed. She was too smart for that. "Hey, was that a flash of a dimple I saw?" she teased him. "Naw, must be sleep deprivation giving me hallucinations."

He responded by leaning forward to flick his white towel at her.

She quickly stepped out of range while warning, "Watch it, buster!" She wagged her index finger at him. "I'm a master towel swatter. You don't want to mess with me. I grew up with two brothers, so my dad taught me how to protect myself."

"With shaving cream and towel swatting?"

"Among other things." A huge yawn caught her unawares, reminding her of her purpose in coming to his door. Not to ogle him, but to keep him quiet. "I need more sleep, so do me a favor and keep your Arnold Schwarzenegger impressions confined to the respectable hours between noon and midnight." She yawned once more before growling à la Arnold, "Hasta la vista, baby."

As David watched her amble downstairs, he couldn't take his eyes off her. He'd never met a woman like her. She certainly had her own way of doing things, and just when he thought he had her pegged, she'd throw him a curveball.

He'd already had a buddy at the police department run a background check on Anastasia. She had one arrest four years ago. She'd been detained, along with twenty other demonstrators, at a sit-in protesting the demolition of a historic building. But that didn't mean she was innocent of any wrongdoing in the meantime. It could just mean that she was too smart to get caught. Yet.

He aimed on changing that. Starting with their picnic later today.

DAVID CHECKED his watch to make sure it was six o'clock on the money. Only then did he lift his hand to knock on Anastasia's front door. But before his knuckles made contact with the wood, the door was yanked open and a wild-eyed Anastasia came rushing out, almost knocking him over in her haste to race downstairs.

"Hey!" Concerned, he rushed after her. "Are you okay?"

She didn't answer and he didn't catch up with her until they were outside, where he found her in the back, by the gravel alley that ran behind the building. She was acting very strangely, turning around in quick circles and nearly tumbling into a line of skinny shrubs as she did so.

"What is this, that tai chi you were talking about? Are you trying to appease the picnic gods or something?" he inquired.

"I'm trying to confuse the mouse," she replied breathlessly.

"Right." The woman was crazy. "It's watching you from the bushes?"

"No, it's right in here." She shoved the mousetrap at him, making him hurriedly back up. It was well-known in the department that he was no fan of mice, or rats, either, for that matter. They gave him the creeps.

"You keep mice?" His voice was raspy as he tried to hide his sweaty palms behind his back.

"No, I'm trying to get rid of it. I'm turning in circles to disorient it so it won't run right back inside." She spun around again then opened the trap and let a dizzy mouse scramble out. Once free, it made an unsteady path toward the garage on the opposite side of the alley.

"Why don't you just kill it?" he demanded. "That would stop it from running back inside."

"My brother Ryan had a white mouse as a pet when we were kids, so I can't kill a mouse without remembering Pescado."

"Pescado?" He frowned. "He had a mouse named Pescado? That's Spanish for fish not mouse."

"I know and so did Ryan, But my brother is perverse that way."

"If you can't kill the mouse, then get a cat and let it do the nasty deed."

"I have a cat," she replied, leaning down to pick up the now-vacated humane trap. "Her name is Xena. But she's afraid of mice."

"What kind of cat is afraid of mice?"

She glared at him, daring him to insult her pet. "*My* kind."

"Figures," he muttered.

"What's that mean?"

"You don't do anything normally."

"Normally, I do a great deal."

It was his turn to glare. He didn't appreciate having his words turned back on him in a grammatical tug-of-war. "You know what I mean."

"If you were attempting to compliment me on my uniqueness, then I thank you," she said with a regal air that was soon ruined by her teasing grin. "If it was anything else, I'd say you were in for a rough evening. Remember that I'll be providing the food, and you don't want to aggravate the cook."

"You cooked?"

"Yes, I cooked. Lower your eyebrows. You don't have to look and sound so surprised about it. I'm a fairly good cook." Glancing at her Swiss railway watch, she said, "We really should get going, we don't want to be late."

Late? he wondered. For a picnic? A second later she was racing back upstairs. Hanging out with her was exercise enough, David decided as he hurried after her. While doing so, he couldn't help noticing and appreciating the way her floral sundress clung to her body in all the right places. She wore a white shirt over top of it, the shirttail tied in a knot around her waist.

She didn't have that skinny flat look that seemed so popular these days. She was more a throwback to Marilyn Monroe. Especially when the full skirt on her dress swirled up around her great legs as she swung around the newel post going two-forty.

By the time he entered her apartment, she was waiting for him. He took a quick look around but only had time to notice that she didn't have much furniture in the room, two flowery stuffed chairs instead of a couch and a wildly colorful strange-looking table. Then his attention turned to the paraphernalia on the floor beside her.

"What is all this?" he asked, suspiciously eyeing the things she'd gathered. "We're only going on a picnic, not a trek in the jungle for a month."

She reassuringly patted his arm the way Claire often did. "We'll need every bit of this, trust me."

That was the problem. He couldn't completely trust her and he couldn't get her out of his mind. He'd heard that the best con artists oozed charm. How about sex appeal? She had plenty of that, too. What was she up to?

"Where exactly are we going?" he asked as he hefted two lawn chairs and a huge plastic cooler.

"Ravinia." She added a long skinny bag beneath his arm. "Have you ever been there?"

He paused. "Don't they play music or something there?"

"Or something," she agreed, tucking her long hair behind one ear as she grabbed two more tote bags. "It's the summer home for the Chicago Symphony Orchestra."

"I suppose it's too much to hope that a David Bowie concert is playing tonight."

"Relax." Another pat, this time on his back. "You're going to have a great time."

"Why are you so worried about me having a good time?"

"Because I think you don't do it enough. Is it okay if we use your Blazer? It holds more than my little red Triumph."

So that spiffy sports car parked out front was hers? What kind of librarian drove a car like that? Before meeting her, he thought they all wore orthopedic shoes and hairnets, and drove sedate sedans. Looking at her sexy purple sandals, he realized that he had a lot to learn about librarians and a lot more to learn about Anastasia in particular. And with a jolt, he realized he really wanted to know.

THEIR CONVERSATION was easygoing as they drove to the nearby suburb of Highland Park, home of the Ravinia Festival. It wasn't a long drive. David was surprised at the number of people who were in the parking lot ahead of them. Many trekked their stuff into the park using luggage carts or kids' red wagons. Anastasia hemmed and hawed about where to settle before finally choosing what she called the perfect spot—on the lawn beneath a stand of oak trees, close enough to the covered pavilion to be able to see the orchestra, or so she told him.

David didn't care about seeing musicians, he wanted to see some food. He was starving. But apparently Anastasia had a routine to follow first. He helped her lay down a blanket on top of what looked like a plastic tarp. After unfolding the two lawn chairs, she handed him the long skinny bag with the request, "Would you put this together for me, please?"

Wondering if this was some kind of trick question or test, he said, "What is it?"

"A table."

Five minutes later, he said, "I hate to tell you this, but someone has trashed your table. They've cut the legs short."

"They're supposed to be short," she replied as she arranged a pastel tablecloth on it before adding several turquoise candles in glass holders.

"Why?"

"To make it easier to carry."

As the one who'd had to haul the table, David had his doubts about short legs being any easier. "Seems like a strange way of having a picnic to me."

"Oh, so now you're an expert on picnics?"

"I know enough." Opening the plastic cooler, he peered inside. "I'm starving. Where's the fried chicken?"

She shuddered. "Do you know what that does to your arteries?"

"I know what it does to my taste buds. I like fried chicken. And you should talk, I hear ice cream isn't exactly artery friendly."

"I'd rather have ice cream than fried chicken."

"What kind of picnic has stunted tables, candles and no fried chicken?"

"Calm down. I've got plenty of goodies. Here, try some dip to get you started." He went through that in about five minutes.

"Sorry to be such a pig." He gave her a chagrined smile even as he licked a bit of soft cheese from his index finger. "It's just that I haven't eaten anything all day."

"Here, have some more crackers." She handed him the box. "Give me a minute to set up." She pulled a glass vase and some fresh flowers from one of the tote bags. Using bottled water, she filled the vase and set it in the middle of the table.

"Seems like a lot of work for a picnic."

"It's a tradition here at Ravinia," she informed him.

Looking around, David had to admit that they weren't the only ones with a fancy layout.

"Okay, I've got some chilled avocado soup for the first course, followed by potato and beet salad, carrot salad, and..." Pulling a thermal case from the tote bag, she said, "Ta-da! Warm baked chicken. Plus some of your grandmother's homemade pistachio ice cream for dessert."

By the time the concert started at eight, he and Anastasia were sitting side by side on lawn chairs, and he was feeling more mellow. The food had been great, if unusual to a man more accustomed to eating takeout.

And she was right, most of the surrounding crowd did have candles set out on their blankets or tables, apparently as a deterrent to mosquitoes as well as for atmosphere. The classical music was loud and emotional, not something you could dance to, but it didn't grate on his nerves. In fact, he sort of liked it.

He also liked the way couples made themselves

comfortable on their blankets, women leaning their heads on their guys' shoulders. David was about to suggest Anastasia join him on the blanket when she tapped him on the shoulder and nodded over her shoulder.

Turning, he saw the last remnants of a crimson sunset and the flickering of hundreds of candles to the farthest edges of the park.

"Nice, huh?" she whispered.

"Not bad," he agreed.

Anastasia hoped that his words meant that he was finally having a good time. She'd been doubtful at first, but he seemed to have settled in just fine now. Maybe he'd been cranky earlier because he was hungry.

Normally, at this point in the evening, she'd stretch out on the blanket and wrap it around her as the night air turned a bit chilly. But David seemed like a picnic-table or lawn-chair kind of guy, although the jeans and denim shirt he was wearing did give him the casual appearance of a man comfortable in his own skin. Maybe she'd misjudged him by thinking he couldn't relax.

Instead of saying anything, she simply abandoned her lawn chair for the blanket, leaving it up to him whether or not to join her. He did, with surprising alacrity. He stretched out so close beside her that she could feel his body heat.

Feeling awkward, suddenly unsure where to put her arms and hands, she had to smile as David muttered something like "Stop wiggling" and scooted her closer. Her body was now pressed against his side, her head on his shoulder, his arm around her shoulder. It all felt amazingly right.

She barely had time to register that fact before the first raindrops began to fall. The clouds that had made the sunset so stunning were now overhead. A few wimps in the audience hurriedly gathered up their stuff and left, but a majority stayed and simply brought out the umbrellas.

Anastasia would have done that, too, but she'd left her umbrella at home.

"Don't worry," she reassured David as she sat up and tugged the blanket and tarp out from under him. "I'm an experienced Ravinia-goer. I know what to do."

"Leave?" he suggested hopefully.

"No." She sat in a lawn chair, now placed directly on the grass, and patted the chair beside her. As David joined her, she handed him the opposite corner of the plastic tarp. He frowned at the ridiculously colorful penguins printed on it.

"It's an old shower curtain," she explained as she held the tarp over her head with one hand and spread the blanket over their knees with the other. "We can still listen to the music. Luckily, the rain held off until intermission. I love this next piece. It's Rimsky-Korsakov's *Scheherazade*." Reading from the damp program in her hands, she said, "The Sultan Schahriar, convinced of the duplicity and infidelity of all women—male chauvinist pig that he is..."

David tried to read over her shoulder. "It says that?"

"Okay, I added the pig part," she confessed.

"Anyway, he vowed to slay each of his wives after his first night with them. The Sultana Scheherazade saved her life by telling the sultan a series of continuing stories over a period of a thousand and one nights. Overcome by curiosity, each day the monarch postponed her execution to hear the next part of the tale, until in the end he gave Scheherazade her life."

David didn't think it was a coincidence that Anastasia so loved Scheherazade. One storyteller relating to another. Even if she'd done nothing else wrong, she'd filled his grandmother's head with unrealistic expectations and put Claire's retirement security at risk. Clearly Anastasia was a bad influence. Why, just the other day, he'd actually caught his grandmother— a lifelong Lawrence Welk fan—listening and bouncing to Bruce Springsteen's "Born in the U.S.A." Anastasia's influence, no doubt. Filling his grandmother with wild ideas.

And filling him with...what? What did he call this feeling? Interest? Lust? Aggravation? He preferred to focus on the latter.

After all, he'd missed a Cubs game to be here with her. And while those few minutes with her lush body pressed against his had been worth missing a baseball game for, he wished the experience had lasted longer.

"So," she asked cheerfully, "are you having fun yet?"

"Yeah, right." It couldn't get much worse than this, could it?

It could. The itching started as they made their way back to his black Blazer in the farthest corner of the parking lot. He had to pause several times en route to scratch his arms and the back of his neck. "Do they have poison ivy in this park?" he asked.

"No."

With dismay, he eyed the welts that were forming on his arms. "What did you put in the food?"

"Nothing suspicious."

"Any shrimp?"

She nodded. "Yes, there was some shredded shrimp in the dip."

"That's it. I'm allergic to shrimp. They give me hives."

"I'm so sorry! You should have told me. How severe is your allergy? Do you need to take some kind of medication? Should we go to a hospital?"

"No," he admitted. "All I need is an antihistamine."

"While I did want to make this evening one you wouldn't forget, this wasn't quite what I had in mind," she said apologetically.

"Me, neither."

"So, maybe we should do it again sometime soon, huh?" Her grin was irreverent and contagious.

"Maybe we should," he agreed. "Only this time I'll show you *my* version of a great time."

"Which is?"

"Baseball."

And so it was that Anastasia ended up at Wrigley Field the very next afternoon.

"I wasn't sure we could get in," David said. He'd completely recovered from his allergic reaction of the night before. "You're lucky I was able to get us two tickets on such short notice."

"Hmm, right. Lucky. People must be lining up to see a team that hasn't won a World Series since 1908."

"I thought you said you didn't know anything about baseball." He took her arm to help her down the concrete steps to their bleacher seats.

"I'm a librarian. Information is my specialty."

His specialty seemed to be making her heart hum. She was also starting to really like the sound of his voice, the unique golden-gruff texture of it. Too bad she didn't like most of what he said during the drive to what natives referred to as Wrigleyville. He'd tried to give her a lecture on the advantages of responsibility and the foolhardiness of dreams

"What do you have against dreams anyway?" she demanded as she followed him down an aisle.

He frowned at her. "Where did that come from?"

"Our conversation on the drive over here. Come on, tell me."

"Dreams are a waste of time. Even worse, they can be dangerous."

"How so?"

"Because they can blind you to reality and leave you unprepared for the future."

"Are you referring to your grandmother? I know you're worried about her retirement security, but..."

"I was talking about my parents," he said curtly. "My dad risked everything for his dream of getting rich fast. It isn't the dreamers who pay, it's the rest of their family." His face darkened before he shrugged. "Let's just say that I'm a practical man. I don't believe in the Easter Bunny or a pot of gold at the end of a rainbow. So sue me.''

"What do you believe in?"

"Hard work and baseball," he replied. "Now tell me, how could you grow up with two brothers and never have gone to a baseball game?"

"Just lucky, I guess. So you think dreams are dangerous because of your dad?"

"And because I've seen too many dreams go up in smoke," he growled. "You won't find many dreamers in my line of work."

She nodded slowly. "I suppose I can understand that." David wasn't the kind of man to open up easily, and if she kept pushing him he'd just get crabby...or crabbier. The telltale flash of irritation was already apparent in his to-die-for blue eyes. She'd learned enough for now. Smiling at him, she said, "And to answer your questions about my not going to a game before, my dad likes the Cubs, but he mostly watches them on TV, while my brothers prefer basketball and the Bulls."

"And you? What do you prefer?"

"The ballet." Settling into her seat, she sniffed the air. The day was sunny, with a crisp breeze off the lake that reminded her that September was only a few days away. "You know, I thought a baseball game would smell differently."

He looked at her as if she were crazy. "What?"

"You know, smell less like fresh air and more like hot dogs and mustard."

"It smells like that by the concession stands. The hot-dog sellers don't bring any mustard with them out here. It's been my experience that their hot dogs are cold and their beer warm.''

She grimaced. ''Yummy.''

''I brought a bag of peanuts for us to shell. Want some?'' His fingers brushed hers as he held out a handful for her to take. Turning her free hand palm up, he transferred the peanuts from his hand to hers. A murmur of awareness flowed from his touch.

She looked up and their gazes connected. She liked the way he wore his baseball cap backward so that the brim didn't shield his eyes from her. You'd think she would have gotten over their incredible color by now, but no, she was as fascinated as ever.

She welcomed the opportunity to distract herself from David's potent allure when it was time to sing the national anthem, but from there things went downhill fast, or should she say *slow*. Excruciatingly slow. She was bored senseless.

David, however, showed no signs of being bored.

''This guy throws a knuckle curve,'' he leaned over to tell her what felt like an hour later.

''Which guy?''

''The pitcher.''

''He's the one out on that little hill, right?''

David frowned. ''It's called a pitcher's mound.''

The heavyset man on her other side leaped to his feet, jostling her arm and tossing her peanuts two rows forward. When the disgruntled people in that row turned to give her a dirty look, she scrunched down in her seat. Which didn't make it any more comfortable. Resting on the ground at Ravinia was more comfortable than this.

"Here." David handed her the large bag of peanuts. "Help yourself to some more. Keeps you busy while nothing is going on in the game."

"Which is quite often, from what I've seen," she muttered.

"It's only the fourth inning. You haven't seen a heck of a lot."

"You can say that again."

Everyone leaped to their feet once again. Everyone except Anastasia, who had a lapful of peanuts. She'd worn jeans and a T-shirt, figuring that would be good attire for a baseball game. Her cap said Reading Is Fundamental instead of bearing a logo like the ones on the caps of the rest of the audience.

By the time she got her lap cleared, everyone was in their seats again. She was better prepared the next time the crowd leaped to their feet. By the time the seventh-inning stretch came around, she'd found her rhythm.

"You know the best thing about this game?" she said.

David nodded. "That we're only down by a pair."

"A pair of what?"

He frowned again. "The score is two to four."

"I knew that." She munched on a peanut before adding, "The best part about this game is singing 'Take Me Out To The Ball Game' during the seventh-inning stretch. Oh, and yelling whatever you want during the game."

"What are you talking about?"

"You can stand up and say anything and nobody

notices. Watch this.'' Getting up with the rest of the crowd, she yelled, ''Rutabagas are dumb veggies.''

He yanked her back down into her seat. ''Stop that!''

''Why? Nobody paid any attention.''

Next time, she stood and yelled, ''Attrition stinks!''

When she sat down, the bald guy in the row behind shouted, ''Attrition, he's their shortstop, right?''

Grinning at David, Anastasia said, ''*Now* I'm having fun.''

5

"Do you think we're going to be finished in time for the grand opening?" Claire asked David as he took a break from his renovation work. The place was really torn up now that they were well into the second week of the project. The smell of plywood and plumbing compound mixed with the aromas of coffee and doughnuts.

"I think so," David replied. "I've just gone over the plans with the plumber and the electrician. They should be finished with their work by the beginning of next week, and then the heating people are coming in, but they'll be wrapping things up a few days later."

"The place looks much bigger now that you've torn down those two walls, doesn't it?"

David nodded absently, his thoughts on the discovery he'd made as a result of removing those non-load-bearing walls. Something didn't jibe. He'd gotten the building's floor plans when he'd applied for a building permit, so he knew where the walls were supposed to be. The problem was, there was a three-foot discrepancy between the outer basement wall and the rest of the building.

The same morning he'd gotten the building permit,

he'd also checked out the title history of the property to make sure that the sale had been aboveboard regarding ownership and clear title. In doing so, he'd discovered that the place had once belonged to Chester "Chesty" Ferguson, the proprietor of a very prosperous speakeasy during Prohibition in the 1920s.

David had had an interest in that colorful era in Chicago's history ever since he was a kid, watching the adventures of Elliot Ness in reruns of "The Untouchables." Under other circumstances he might have dismissed a three-foot discrepancy between the outer walls in the basement and those in the rest of the building as an error in the blueprints, a simple miscalculation on someone's part. But given that the place had once been a speakeasy, he couldn't help wondering about the possibility of a hidden storage room down there.

So far he'd only had time to make a cursory inspection of the basement. There was too much work to be done on the main level and it had to be done in time for the October first opening his grandmother was counting on.

"Do you regret agreeing to help me with this project?" Claire suddenly asked him, her expression one of concern. "I'm not sure you knew what you were getting into."

"I knew. And I have no regrets, except that you bought the building without consulting me first."

"I knew you wouldn't agree, wouldn't see the place as I do. But I think perhaps you're beginning to now, hmm?"

David grunted a noncommittal reply. Even he had

to admit that the storefront was starting to show some promise. He'd stripped layers of paint and decades of grime from the walls, wood moldings and trim to reveal their natural beauty. The walls had oak wainscoting with clean lines and excellent detailing.

The marble countertop had been covered with a thick dropcloth all this time, to protect it from the workmen. His grandmother checked the countertop twice a day to make sure it was still okay. The floor was also covered to protect the tile. During the construction, dust was everywhere, but that hadn't kept Claire from spending most afternoons here to check things out.

"So, have you decided what to call the place?" he asked.

Claire shook her head. "Not yet."

"I don't see what's wrong with The Scoop Coop."

"It's too much of a tongue twister. It sounds a bit awkward to say, 'Let's go to The Scoop Coop.'" Claire checked her list before casually saying, "By the way, I've been meaning to tell you, I'm so glad that you and Anastasia are getting along better and actually having fun together."

David rolled his eyes. "You make it sound like we're a pair of twelve-year-olds playing in the backyard."

"Nonsense, dear." She patted his arm. "I can assure you that I'm very much aware that you're both adults and that time is quickly marching right on by."

David was aware of time passing, as well. It had been five days since he'd taken Anastasia to her first baseball game. Since then he'd only seen her in passing, when she dropped by after work to consult with his grandmother about everything from wallpaper to soda-fountain glassware. Much as he hated to admit it, he missed her and wished she was around more.

No sooner had the thought crossed his mind than he heard her voice coming from directly behind him.

"Daydreaming on the job again, Sullivan?" she teased.

Turning to face her, he said, "How can you sneak up on me like that wearing combat boots?"

"What, you don't like my choice in footwear?" Lifting her right foot, she swiveled it for his perusal. "I had no idea you were such a slave to fashion," she added, eyeing his worn jeans and dusty white T-shirt.

"Yeah, right." He couldn't help himself. He smiled.

"I saw that. You're trying to distract me again with those sexy dimples of yours, but it's not going to work," she assured him. "I'm here to tell Claire that I found a manufacturer in Chicago who makes soda-fountain and dipping cabinets to order." She turned to Claire. "I got the information out of a book on the history of ice cream, so I photocopied the page for you, Claire."

Claire nodded and smiled.

"The history of ice cream?" David repeated.

"You bet. And if you're a good boy, someday I might tell you about it."

"I'll be waiting with bated breath."

Anastasia was very much aware of the teasing note in his voice and the gleam in his blue eyes. The more she heard him speak, the more she enjoyed listening to him as she mentally tried to decipher what exactly it was about his voice that intrigued her so. Was it the way he gently rolled his H's, or his slightly lazy drawl, or the simple golden resonance of it? She couldn't be sure.

One thing she did know, he still didn't trust her completely. But to give him credit, he'd been relatively nice to her anyway. He'd been a good sport about their Ravinia experience and about her own antics at the baseball game. While he still grumbled about the impracticality of opening an ice-cream parlor, she could tell that his protests lacked their earlier forcefulness. She'd even heard that he'd come up with a name of his own for the place, The Scoop Coop. Now if she could only get him to admit that dreams were a good thing, then her mission would be accomplished.

"HOW ARE YOU going to get these two married when they haven't even kissed yet?" Betty was marching across the dust-covered marble countertop like an impatient marine.

"They're building the anticipation," Hattie replied from midair, where she daintily batted her gossamer wings in order to hover.

"I have to agree with Betty on this one." Muriel shook her head, making her cowlick stick up even more than usual. "Jason and Ryan had already kissed their soul mates by now."

Hattie gave her sisters a reprimanding look. "Anastasia marches to her own drummer, you both should know that by now.''

''I thought that using Claire was supposed to speed things along,'' Muriel said.

Hattie shook her head and almost knocked her cherry-red pillbox hat off. ''I don't recall Betty saying anything about speed. As I remember it, she said that enlisting Claire's assistance would give us more time to take care of our other charges and would make this case a piece of cake. Of course, right after Betty said that, Anastasia pushed that beastly jerk into the wedding cake.''

''Which should have been my first hint that things wouldn't go smoothly,'' Betty muttered.

''They never do. You said it was more of a challenge this way,'' Hattie reminded her.

''I lied,'' Betty said.

''Fiddlesticks!'' Hattie replied. ''I think you're both worrying needlessly. Things are going well. David doesn't distrust Anastasia as much as he did in the beginning. He may be confused by his attraction to her, but he's not being as bad as he could be. And Anastasia is seeing definite promise in David. Did you notice how she teased him about her boots and about the history of ice cream?''

''What's there to tease about the history of ice cream?'' Muriel asked. ''Everyone knows that ice cream was created by fairy godmothers once upon a time.''

''Actually, the human history books say that the origins of ice cream are shrouded in mystery,'' Hattie said.

Muriel shrugged. "That's just their way of saying fairy godmothers created it."

"Maybe that's what Anastasia is going to tell him."

"Right," Betty scoffed. "And if you believe that, I've got a bridge to sell you."

"No, thank you." Hattie's voice was prim and proper. "I'm not into bridges."

Muriel, as usual, had the last word. "The only thing I know about bridges is that we'd better not burn any behind us."

"ARE YOU SURE you're ready for this?" David asked Anastasia a week later. "It's an important step to take."

"We've waited long enough," she replied breathlessly. "I'm ready. Now give me that roller." She grabbed it out of his hand. "We've got a lot of walls to paint."

"Are you sure this is how you want to spend your day off?"

"Absolutely." Rearranging the wide straps on her painter's overalls, she shot him a saucy look. "Why? Are you afraid I'm a better painter than you are?"

"Yeah, I'm just trembling in my boots," he retorted mockingly.

"Fighting words, Mr. Construction Man. Get your roller and prepare to meet your better."

"Better what?"

"Better get moving, you're behind already."

And while she was at it, she noted how sexy his behind looked, covered by the worn denim of his jeans. Maybe it was those jumping jacks he did, although, thankfully, not at five in the morning any longer. Or maybe it was just good genes. She could get used to having him around. How did that phrase go…something about being easy on the eyes. And speaking of eyes, the blue paint Claire had chosen matched his eyes almost exactly.

The grin he shot her way made her pause, which in turn gave him time to catch up with her. After that, she focused on the job at hand. They passed the time exchanging quips as David's boom box played a shuffle of hits from the eighties, running the gamut from Kenny Loggins to David Bowie to Cyndi Lauper.

Anastasia had finished her designated wall and was using a brush to do the edges while bopping to "Girls Just Want to Have Fun" when she inadvertently splattered her brush during one particularly enthusiastic dance step. Unfortunately she splattered it in David's direction, scoring a direct hit on the right shoulder of his white T-shirt.

Putting her hand to her mouth, she said, "Oops."

"Oops doesn't cut it," he growled with pretend menace. "This was the last clean T-shirt I had left since I started this project. I'll show you oops." He advanced toward her like a man bent on revenge.

She hastily retreated like a woman bent on not getting caught. "Okay, now," she said in a placating voice, "let's think about this before you do something you might regret."

"Oh, I don't think I'll have any regrets. You might, though."

"It was an accident, I swear." She held her free hand to her chest as she made the vow. Then she added, "If I'd really been trying to hit you, I would have done a better job of it."

"Like this, you mean?" He zapped her, splattering blue paint in the middle of the orange cropped top she wore beneath her overalls.

"Hey, two can play at that game, buddy!" This time she was the one who advanced, while he retreated.

"I think we should be adults and call it even now."

"Easy for you to say." Using her brush the way a fencer would use a rapier, she put her left hand in the air à la Errol Flynn. "En garde!"

He was so busy laughing that she easily got in a swipe on his bare arm.

That caught his attention. "Now you've done it."

The next thing she knew, he'd grabbed her in his arms. Her laughter ceased when, in her teasing struggle to get free, her lips came within millimeters of his.

Lowering his head, he covered her mouth with his own. There was none of the tentativeness that normally went with a first kiss. Instead there was a sultry rightness about it all—from the taste of him to the erotic way he teasingly caught her bottom lip between his teeth.

The kiss was long and lingering. Anastasia was stunned by the passion he evoked within her. Did he know that? Could he feel it, too?

Her hands rested on his chest, put there originally to prevent him from splattering paint on her, but now…now she clenched her fingers into the softness of his white T-shirt with catlike pleasure. She could feel his heart pounding beneath her palm.

So she wasn't the only one affected. Then it was over as quickly as it had begun. She wondered why David had pushed her away, before realizing they weren't alone any longer. The heating contractor and his assistant had returned from their lunch break and were tromping through on their way to the basement.

Trying to keep her equilibrium despite the fact that she was shaken, Anastasia shot David a brilliant smile as she said, "Nice try at distracting me, but I'm still a better painter than you are."

"You're not a bad kisser, either."

"Thanks." Her voice shook. The kiss made her look at him in a new way, a way that made her feel less in control of the situation. And that was something she couldn't cope with at the moment, so she picked up her paintbrush and got back to work, adding a flippant, "But flattery will get you nowhere."

David kissing her until her kneecaps melted, however, could get her in *big* trouble. And she knew it. She was afraid that now he knew it, too.

DAVID WASN'T SURE what prompted him to drop by the library where Anastasia was employed. But then he hadn't been himself all day. That kiss they'd shared yesterday had thrown him for a loop. Who could have known that she could kiss like that? Was it her way of distracting him from his mission of discovering what she was really up to?

What if she wasn't up to anything? That thought had started to cross his mind a time or two lately.

Maybe she was just naive, enthusiastic and impractical? Maybe she wasn't conning his grandmother. But that didn't mean that she was the woman for him. He stopped himself. Where had that thought come from? He and Anastasia were much too different.

Maybe seeing her in her own environment would give him some perspective. The particular branch of the Chicago Public Library where she worked was located in what looked more like a storefront than a library. He had no trouble finding the children's section, he just followed the reading-rainbow mural on the wall until he reached the Munchkin-size table and chairs.

He had no trouble spotting Anastasia. She was in the middle of a crowd of twenty-five preschoolers. Today her long brown hair was in a single braid down her back. She was wearing a denim jumper over a red T-shirt and she was reading the kids a funny book about a frog who, when kissed by a prince, turned into a beautiful librarian.

Of course that got him thinking about the incredible kiss he'd shared with Anastasia, and a good five minutes went by before he came back to earth. By then, Anastasia had gone on to another story. In her hands were a series of large laminated drawings as she spun the tale of a trio of fairy godmothers who wished they had bigger wings.

"Henrietta, Betina and Maria love to laugh. Can you laugh?" Anastasia asked the kids.

They did, with varying enthusiasm.

"They also love ice cream. Do you love ice cream?"

Most shouted their enthusiasm, but one little girl disdainfully said, "It's fattening."

"Not to fairy godmothers, Mitsy," Anastasia replied, not missing a beat. "But today our godmothers have a job to do. They need to help Princess Sarah find her lost kitten. Can you find the kitten in this picture?"

Several kids came forward to point to the corner of the illustration.

"Kittens scratch people and couches." This from Mitsy.

"Since fairy godmothers can fly," Anastasia continued, "they checked the treetops first. Maybe the kitten had climbed a tree. Can you point to the tree in this picture?"

"Trees have bugs." Mitsy shuddered.

Anastasia didn't miss a beat. "They saw lots of birds, but no kitten. So they asked Robbie the Robin if he had seen the kitten."

"Birds poop on cars," Mitsy said.

David was tempted to tell the kid to lighten up, but Anastasia appeared to be used to the child's gloomy comments.

"The fairy godmothers were getting worried. How do you look when you're worried?" The group made faces, wrinkling their noses and foreheads. The little complainer didn't have to do anything, her perpetual expression was already pretty close to a frown.

When Anastasia smiled encouragingly at one of the kids, David was momentarily distracted by the curve of Anastasia's mouth and the memory of their kiss. Where had she learned to kiss like that? Not from any book, that's for sure. Which meant what? That she had a lot of experience? Or she just had great natural talent?

Frowning, he tried to focus on her words instead of her luscious mouth.

"Then they used their magic wands to part the leaves from the trees," she was saying. "They made the wind blow."

"Leaves are messy," Mitsy said with a sniff.

"And on the tallest tree, hiding beneath the leaves, was the little kitten Smitten. Now Smitten was afraid to come down from that tree. So do you know what the fairy godmothers did?"

"Shoot her?" suggested one redheaded boy with bloodthirsty glee.

"No, of course not!" Anastasia gave him a reprimanding look. "That would hurt the kitten and you don't ever want to hurt a kitten or shoot at anything."

"They used magic," a little boy said around the thumb stuck halfway in his mouth.

"That's right, Bobby! They used their magic wands to bring the kitten down from the tree and back to Princess Sarah. The fairy godmothers who thought they were so strange because they had little wings were now heroes. The princess was so happy to have her kitten back that do you know what she gave the fairy godmothers?"

"Lotsa money?" the bloodthirsty little redheaded kid suggested.

"She gave them a day off," David offered.

Anastasia looked surprised to see him as he stepped out from behind the reading tree that had partially hidden him from view. But she continued with her story. "She gave them the gift of laughter and confidence."

"If she laughs like you, it's not a bad gift," he said huskily.

"Oh, yuck, they're gonna get mushy and kissy-faced," the redhead terror exclaimed.

"No, we're not," Anastasia said in what David assumed was her librarian's voice. "I'll be with you in a minute, David." First she completed the rest of her story routine with a hand puppet named Miss Mouse, and only when the preschoolers were returned to their parents did she return her attention to David. "What are you doing here?"

"I thought I'd drop by and see what you do for a living. Singing and telling stories. Not a bad gig."

"It is a good gig, but I do a lot more than sing and read stories. I also work at the reference desk, answering kids' questions, like what animals live in South America, for example, and I recommend books for them to read for fun. I also make administrative decisions, come up with new programs and projects. You have to really like kids for this job," she said ruefully, "it's not something you can learn."

The thought of her and kids made him wonder what kind of mom she'd be. Don't think about that, his bachelor inner voice warned him. Dangerous territory.

"So what animals live in South America?" he inquired.

"Capuchin, howler, and woolly monkeys, also vicuna, the anaconda snake. I only know that because I got seven questions in a row on this topic yesterday.

I also had a fourth-grader who wanted a photograph of a dinosaur and was most upset when I couldn't produce one.''

"Have him contact Steven Spielberg."

"Right." She straightened her stack of poster board–size illustrations.

"What book are these from?"

"They're not from a book. I drew them myself."

"They're not bad," he noted in surprise. "Not that I'm any expert on this stuff or anything."

"Thanks." A moment later, Anastasia had to excuse herself to help a mother looking for a book for her son to read. As Anastasia went to her desk to type something on the computer keyboard, David was struck by how...professional she seemed. He used computers at times, but he never felt comfortable doing it. She looked perfectly at ease.

Here at the library she didn't seem ditzy or crazy or intent on driving him nuts with her sexy smile and teasing laughter. Here she seemed like a brainy woman, the type he'd avoided in the past.

He was willing to admit he may have been off base about her trying to con his grandmother. But that didn't change the fact that she was a classy librarian while he was a burnt-out arson investigator going through an identity crisis.

When she returned to his side, he said, "Have you noticed that we don't have a lot in common?"

"Where did that come from?" she said, sounding surprised.

He shrugged. "You're a classy librarian who likes

symphonies and ballet. I'm a regular working stiff who likes baseball and the Three Stooges.''

"Do you prefer Shemp or Curly?" she stunned him by asking.

"Curly."

"Soitenly," she said, mimicking the comics' routine. "And how many comics were actually part of the Three Stooges?"

"Six. What's Larry's surname?" he shot back.

"Fine. Larry Fine."

"Right." His look reflected how impressed he was. "You're good."

"So I've been trying to tell you," she retorted with a saucy grin.

Shaking his head, he admitted, "I've never met a woman who liked the Three Stooges."

"Ah, but then you've never met a woman like me."

"I'm starting to think you may be right about that," he murmured.

"I'm always right," she noted with an irreverent grin.

"I HOPE YOU DON'T MIND that I've invited David to come with us to the flea market today," Claire said to Anastasia the following afternoon.

"No, I don't mind." It was the first Saturday in September and they were driving out to the Kane Country Flea Market in St. Charles, about ninety minutes southwest of Chicago, to look for more fixtures for the ice-cream parlor.

"Good. I'm glad to hear that. I'm also glad to see

that you were as good as your word and you managed to turn David around and teach him how to have fun. Have you noticed how much more relaxed he seems?''

Anastasia nodded. She'd noticed plenty about David. She'd seen how good he was with his grandmother. She'd been wrong about that. She'd seen how he had a solid core of responsibility. When he said he'd do something, he did it.

The guys she'd been dating were fun-loving but irresponsible. She was starting to think there might be something to be said for a guy who actually did what he said he would, a guy who kissed like there was no tomorrow, a guy with incredible blue eyes and a golden-gruff voice.

''You two ready to go?''

His voice startled her. The jeans and sunshine-yellow Indian cotton shirt she was wearing had seemed fine when it was just her and Claire, but now she worried about how she looked in David's eyes. Not a good sign, she warned herself. You don't want some guy telling you how to dress.

As David drove his Blazer south on Interstate 294 to Interstate 88, Anastasia kept the conversation casual and breezy. Claire had insisted on sitting in the back seat. If Anastasia hadn't known her better, she would have suspected that Claire was trying to matchmake. Surely not. Claire knew how much Anastasia valued her independence.

Anastasia decided the day was too beautiful to worry about anything. The farther west they went, the farther away from the city and its pollutants, the more intense the blue sky became.

The flea market took place on the Kane County Fairgrounds. Outside the entrance gates, farmers from Michigan and Wisconsin were selling bags of fresh-picked apples and apple cider. Inside the fairgrounds, row upon row of vendors were selling everything from factory-direct down comforters to stained-glass windows.

The indoor vendors were located in tin-roofed buildings with signs labeling them as Sheep 1965 or Pigs 1960. The animal stalls had been turned into individual booths, one displaying chinaware, the next containing bolts of material, the next selling shelves of Christmas crafts. Other vendors displayed cases of old jewelry and a large assortment of furniture, both handmade and restored.

Anastasia was the designated navigator. "I heard there's a dealer out here who might have a mirrored back bar," she said. "Something like that would look beautiful on the wall behind the marble counter."

They made a few stops along the way. Anastasia couldn't resist buying a fennel cake hot off the griddle. David looked as if he couldn't resist the dusting of powdered sugar that clung to her lips, but the only thing he indulged in buying was a Three Stooges poster.

Once he had his find safely in hand, David told her, "Most women don't get the Three Stooges' humor."

Anastasia socked his arm. "That's a sexist thing to say. My brother Ryan introduced me to the Three

Stooges when we were kids, but my brother Jason didn't get it. He still doesn't.''

"Is he older than you are?''

"Only by a few minutes, not that you'd ever know that by the way he tried to boss Ryan and I around when we were kids. We were actually all born the same year and day.''

"And you managed that by…?''

"Being triplets.''

Her reply stopped him in his tracks. "Triplets?''

"That's right. My parents had been trying to have kids for a while with no luck. Then they went to a fertility specialist and, as my dad puts it, it worked. The only tough part was growing up with one bathroom and two brothers who hogged it.''

In his investigation of her background, he'd noticed that she had two brothers, but hadn't paid attention to their ages or birth dates. He had noted that one worked for the U.S. Attorney's office in Chicago and the other was a deputy U.S. marshal, so apparently larceny hadn't run in the family. He no longer really believed it ran in Anastasia, either. She was too blunt to con anyone. That didn't mean that he thought she was a good influence on his grandmother, though.

She might not be a swindler, but she was a dreamer and David knew firsthand how harmful that could be. He wasn't ready to give his stamp of approval to Anastasia or this project. True his grandmother seemed to have done her financial homework, but the ice-cream parlor was still an economic risk. And he had no idea what wild idea Anastasia might come up with next.

When they found the booth they'd been looking for, David observed that Anastasia let his grandmother make up her own mind about buying the mirrored-bar thingamajig. He could tell that Claire wanted it. The thing really was huge. He doubted it would even fit in his Blazer, but the dealer said he delivered.

As David took a closer look at the Victorian piece, he figured that it would indeed fill that back wall in the storefront nicely. And the workmanship was good. They didn't make things like this anymore. He then proceeded to bargain with the dealer for a good price, including free delivery.

As the dealer wrote up the order, David finally registered Anastasia and Claire's surprised looks, and said, "What? If you're going to be in business, you might as well get the best price. It's not like money grows on trees, you know."

"I know," Anastasia murmured, laughter and appreciation evident in her voice. "I just didn't think I'd see you so fired up about an old ice-cream parlor fixture."

"As long as you don't get used to it," he grumbled.

6

AS LONG AS YOU don't get used to it. David's words immediately echoed in Anastasia's head with stunning emphasis. The problem was that she *was* getting used to it—used to having him around, used to teasing him, used to kissing him. This feeling was starting to go far beyond merely teaching him how to dream and have fun. What was she getting herself into here?

"Are you okay?" David asked Anastasia as she suddenly stopped in her tracks. "You look funny."

"I'm fine," she lied, fanning her face with her hand and willing her inner panic away. "It's warm in here though. I think I'll head back outside into the fresh air and maybe get a cold lemonade to cool me off."

Looking at David as she spoke was a mistake and only heated her up again. He was wearing jeans and the same denim shirt he'd had on the first time she'd met him. Now, as then, his shirt sleeves were rolled up, displaying his tanned arms. The amount of physical labor he'd been doing in the storefront's restoration showed just a bit in the delineated muscles of his forearms, but it took a keen eye to notice it.

Anastasia had that keen eye where he was concerned, and that worried her. All along, the idea had been to teach David how to loosen up, to show him how to have fun, how to dream. And while their trip to Ravinia hadn't gone the way she'd planned, David *was* showing signs of lightening up. He didn't complain as much about how foolish Claire had been to buy the building, how many businesses failed in their first year, and that sort of thing.

And he certainly didn't kiss like a guy who was a stick-in-the-mud, that's for sure!

"You do look flushed, dear," Claire noted, looking concerned. "I hope you're not coming down with something."

"I hope so, too," she muttered. She'd better not be coming down with David-infatuation, because as great as the guy kissed, he still didn't accept or trust her a hundred percent.

"Do you feel faint?" David asked, putting his arm around her waist as if fearing she might melt on the spot.

His nearness only made her feel hotter. "I just need lemonade."

"Not ice cream?" he teasingly asked.

"It wouldn't be as good as Claire's," Anastasia replied. "She's spoiled me."

"She's good at that."

Anastasia's eyes met his in what was intended to be a brief glance but what blossomed into something much deeper. She found herself becoming fascinated by the darkening hues in his eyes. The irises weren't simply one shade of blue, but a reflection of many hues. His gaze was equally complex, revealing first humor then awareness followed by…could that be…hunger?

Anastasia had no idea how long they stood there staring at each other like lovesick fools before the sound of Claire's voice brought them back to planet Earth. She prayed it was only a second or two, not the ten minutes it felt like.

"Oh, look," Claire exclaimed. "There's that nice Mr. Rozenkrantz. Maybe he'd like to join us for some lemonade."

"Who's Mr. Rozenkrantz?" David demanded as his grandmother took off after the man, down the aisle toward the open area outside the building.

"He owns the antique store next door to our building," Anastasia replied, feeling more on solid ground now that they were in the fresh air. "Surely you've noticed it? The Den of Antiquity?"

"No, I never noticed it. What's my grandmother doing?"

"Well, this is just a wild guess here," Anastasia replied, her voice mocking, "but it looks like she's talking to Mr. Rozenkrantz."

"She's doing more than just talking. Look at her batting her eyelashes. She's…she's flirting with him!" He sounded scandalized.

Anastasia couldn't help herself. She laughed.

David was not amused. "What's so funny?"

"You are." She couldn't elaborate further because Claire rejoined them, with a beaming Mr. Rozenkrantz in tow. "Ira, I'd like you to meet my grandson, David. And this is my good friend Anastasia."

"Anastasia I know from her trips into my shop.

How is that handwoven rug working out?'' Ira asked in his booming voice.

"It fits the room perfectly," Anastasia said.

"David." Smiling, Ira stuck out his beefy hand to grab David's and shake it vigorously. "It's good to meet you. Your grandmother here is always singing your praises."

"When did she do that?"

"When she stops by my store for tea in the afternoons."

David's displeasure increased. "And how long has this been going on?"

Anastasia quickly stepped in. "Oh, look," she exclaimed. "There's a camel saddle in that booth over there. I've wanted one for ages. David—" she clamped her hand around his arm "—come with me so you can haggle for the best price on it." She dragged him with her until they were well out of earshot of his grandmother and her male friend.

"What on earth would you need a camel saddle for?" David demanded.

"I don't, although they make nice hassocks for your feet. I just said that to save you from making a fool of yourself."

"Me?" The concept seemed to amaze him.

Eyeing him in exasperation, she said, "You sounded like an angry guardian in a Jane Austen novel." Mimicking his glower, she imitated his tone of voice. "And how long has this been going on?" Resuming her normal voice, she said, "Come on. Your grandmother is an adult. She can have tea with a friend if she wants to."

He glared at her as realization struck. "You've been promoting this, haven't you?"

"Her friendship with Ira? Sure. Why not?"

"Because she's my grandmother, that's why."

"And that prevents her from having a private life?"

"She's in her seventies."

"So is Ira," Anastasia said. "So what?"

Keeping his eagle gaze fixed on Ira, he said, "What's his angle?"

David was starting to really aggravate her now. "What makes you think he's got an angle?"

"Everybody's got an angle," he said.

"Then what's *your* angle?"

"I'm just trying to protect my grandmother."

"From what?"

"From getting hurt. From being taken advantage of."

"The way you thought I was taking advantage of her?"

"I'm not sure you're a good influence on her."

"And you are?"

He seemed stunned by the question. "Of course I am. I only want what's best for her."

"As long as it's what *you* think is best." She felt as if they were back at square one, with David as dense as ever. "If you had your way, she'd never have gotten the chance to realize her dream."

"At the risk of her financial security," he retorted.

Anastasia refused to let that accusation lie. "Do you really think so little of your grandmother? She's a smart cookie. She did her homework. She knows what she's doing.''

''And what she's doing is flirting with that antiques guy. Look at him, he's putting his hand on her shoulder.''

''The Lothario!'' she cried with feigned outrage.

''It's not funny,'' David protested.

''Sure it is.''

''Only because you have a warped sense of humor.''

''It's better than having no sense of humor at all,'' she said, tossing him a superior grin.

''I'm not going to argue with you about this,'' he growled in frustration.

''That's right, you're not. But only because it takes two to argue and I have no intention of getting into that kind of discussion with you.''

''What kind of discussion?''

''The kind you'd lose.'' With a toss of her head, she marched back to Claire and Ira, leaving David stewing.

She couldn't believe how childish he was being about Claire's friendship with Ira. And how distrustful. All his bad traits were coming to the forefront again. After she'd had such hope that he'd been improving, the old David returned.

''So, IRA, how long have you been in business?'' David asked him as he joined them in line for lemonade. ''What?'' he added as both Anastasia and his grandmother glared at him.

''At least wait until the man is sitting down and

sipping his lemonade before you give him the third degree," Anastasia replied. To Ira, she added, "David is an arson investigator. It's his nature to be nosy and suspicious. Don't take it personally."

"I won't," Ira assured her, his brown eyes sparkling with amusement. His white hair might be thinning, but he was still a charmer. "And I've been in business for two years, David."

"That's not very long. Have you always been in the antique business?"

"No, I've tried my hand at a lot of things."

"I'll bet you have," David muttered.

With a steely look of reprimand in David's direction, Claire briskly changed the subject. "I just bought the most beautiful mirrored back bar, Ira, with Tiffany-style lamps at either end and a lovely arched mirror in the center. I can already picture how perfectly at home my tulip-edged parfait glasses will look on the shelves. It's a real gem."

"So are you," Ira murmured gallantly.

"Ever been married, Ira?" David asked with all the subtlety of a bull in a china shop.

"Several times," Ira admitted.

Great. So the guy *was* a womanizer. David had known that there was something fishy about him. And that slippery answer about trying his hand at a lot of things was also suspicious.

"Maybe you should just fingerprint Ira now and get it over with," Anastasia suggested.

David glared at her. Was she blind? Couldn't she see that this Ira was trouble? "I was just making conversation."

"Right." Her expression was one of disbelief.

David quickly realized that he wouldn't be able to get any additional information out of Ira while Claire and Anastasia were on his case. So he bided his time, keeping quiet as Ira and Claire talked about vintage ice-cream scoops and a million other things. He pretended not to be paying attention, but when he later overheard Ira making arrangements to take Claire to dinner that night, David knew what he had to do.

ANASTASIA CHECKED her appearance in the mirror for the fifth time in as many minutes. She looked pretty good. The dress, a vintage design from the 1940s, had a black net top combined with a satin bodice and skirt. She'd found it in a thrift store and hadn't been able to believe her luck. She always felt like Lauren Bacall when she wore it.

Her vivid red lipstick matched the forties mood. Ditto for the jet earrings and bracelet she'd picked up at the flea market that afternoon, after she and David had left Claire with Ira for a few hours.

When David had asked her out to dinner, Anastasia had been tempted to refuse because he'd been such a pill about Ira. But then he'd looked at her so apologetically, oozing sex appeal and remorse, in what turned out to be an irresistible combination for her. She'd caved in like a sand castle hit with a wave.

He arrived at her door precisely on time. In his hand was a single red rose, which he gave her along with a stunning smile. "You look gorgeous," he said appreciatively. "I thought we'd walk to the restaurant since the weather is so great. It isn't far," he added, eyeing her high-heeled shoes.

"These may look good, but first and foremost they're comfortable," Anastasia told him, having belatedly regained her breath. He was wearing a dark suit and a blue-black shirt with a matching tie. The dark colors did wonders for his Black Irish looks. "Walking sounds fine by me."

They walked hand in hand the three blocks to the restaurant he'd chosen. Anastasia knew Rosa's well, it had the best Italian food in the neighborhood. Had David known it was one of her favorite places? She got all warm and fuzzy inside thinking about it, that he'd taken the time to make this evening special, from the rose he'd brought to his selection of the restaurant. It wasn't until they were inside Rosa's that she came down to earth with a bump.

One look at Ira and Claire enjoying a romantic dinner for two was all it took for her to understand what was really going on. Furious, she said, "You lowdown sneak! I'm not staying here and be a partner to your spy mission."

But it was too late. Claire and Ira had already spotted them. "Hey, you two," Ira boomed. "Come on over and join us."

Anastasia shook her head. "We can't—"

"Believe our luck in bumping into you here," David interrupted her. "What a coincidence."

"What a farce," Anastasia muttered. She would have walked out, but she didn't want to upset Claire. She was also determined to protect her friend from her devious grandson. So she stayed. But she was mad, *very* mad.

A waiter brought two more chairs and place settings to the table. Once they had their menus, David said, "So, what do you recommend?"

"Counseling," Anastasia said tartly.

"I don't see it on the menu," David retorted with a warning look.

"Did you two have a fight?" Claire asked, concern marring her expression.

"Not yet," Anastasia replied. "But any minute now…"

Claire frowned at David. "What did you do?"

"Me?" His dark eyebrows rose. "What makes you think it's anything *I* did?"

"Because she knows you," Anastasia said.

Claire patted David's hand. "Yes, dear, I do know you." Anastasia thought she saw a slight grimace cross his face. "Now behave yourself."

Anastasia grinned. Claire, bless her soul, had put David in his place. But being the big galoot that he was, she doubted that he'd take the reprimand to heart for very long. But at least for now Anastasia could enjoy her meal knowing that things had not gone David's way.

"WHAT'S CLAIRE DOING dating?" Hattie was perched on one of the white ceiling fans adorning Rosa's and she was frowning. "I thought her job was to be a matchmaker for Anastasia and David. That should be her focus. I don't get to date." Hattie's frown became a pout. "Why does she?"

"Because she's human and you're not."

"Sure." Hattie sniffed. "Rub it in."

"Oh, get over it." Muriel tossed a crouton at her. The only reason she missed was because Hattie ducked at the last moment.

Straightening her apricot-adorned hat, Hattie checked her reflection in the mirrored compact she'd recently installed at the tip of her magic wand, then said, "I'm just saying that things were going very well between Anastasia and David at the flea market until this Ira fellow showed up and Claire started flirting with him. Now David's distracted by his concern for his grandmother, and Anastasia wants to slug him."

Muriel shrugged. "So we reached a little speed bump in life's superhighway."

Betty shook her head at her sister's phrase and gave her a reprimanding look. "You've been surfing the Internet again, haven't you? I've warned you about visiting those chat rooms."

"I only use it for research. About human behavior and all that," Muriel said defensively.

"Ahem." Hattie loudly cleared her throat. "If we could return to the matter at hand here, namely Anastasia and David. What are we going to do about this?"

"If I were you, I'd get off that ceiling fan," Betty said.

Hattie's expression was haughty. "Why should I?"

"Because someone just turned it on," Betty replied.

An instant later, Hattie was thrown from the fan

clear across the room to land in a heap behind the bar, next to a bottle of Jack Daniel's. Now her hat covered most of her face and the hem of her dress was up around her waist, displaying her colorful bloomers. The force of her landing had dislodged the open bottle of imported sparkling water the bartender had been drinking, tipping it over so that it dripped off the ledge above Hattie onto her upturned face, soaking it.

"First rule of fairy godmothering," Muriel recited. "Never let them see you sweat."

"Okay," David said as he accompanied Anastasia back to her apartment. "So I admit that it wasn't fair of me to include you in my plans to check up on my grandmother—"

Anastasia, who'd been marching ten steps ahead of him, turned on a dime and came back to glare at him with fire in her golden eyes. "I'll tell you what isn't fair. That you…ugh!" She threw her hands up in the air. "I'm too angry to even speak to you right now."

"So I guess this means I won't be getting a good-night kiss when we get back to your apartment, huh?" he asked wryly.

"David, David." Instead of getting angrier with him as he expected, she shook her head at him. "How little you know me."

Uh-oh. David wasn't sure he liked the sound of that.

"Not only will you not be getting a kiss like this…" Tugging him close, she planted a fiery kiss on him right there in the middle of the sidewalk. "But you'll also miss this, as well.'' With her second kiss, she melted against him with such passion that he immediately reached out to embrace her, but she was already gone. She flounced the few yards to their building, after which he could hear the front door slam with enough vehemence to make him wince.

He was in his apartment, nursing his second beer when there was a knock at his door. Thinking it might be Anastasia, he opened the door with some degree of caution and anticipation.

''You look like you were expecting someone else,'' Claire noted.

''Sorry, Gran. Come on in. I suppose you're here to read me the riot act,'' he said, sinking back onto the big soft leather couch that was the only piece of furniture, aside from a state-of-the-art home-entertainment unit, in the living room.

''Of course not, dear.'' Sitting beside him, she patted his hand before reaching for a can of beer and popping it open like a pro.

''You want a glass for that?'' he asked, eyeing her with equal parts of awe and trepidation. He'd never seen his grandmother drink a beer before.

''No, this will be fine. I know you were just concerned about me, and that's why you acted the way you did tonight. And while I appreciate your concern, you really don't have to worry, dear.'' Claire patted his hand again. ''I'd never dream of getting married again.''

Reassured, he took a sip of beer.

''Once you're on social security, it makes much

more sense just to live together,'' she blithely stated. ''Otherwise you lose benefits.''

David choked so badly that Claire had to pound him on the back. ''Oh dear. I've shocked you.''

''Hell, yes!'' he growled.

''Well, dear, you'll just have to live with it,'' she said without an ounce of remorse before adding, ''Don't you worry about me. Focus your attention on Anastasia instead. That's where your future lies.''

His downfall, too, most likely, David thought darkly.

7

"IT'S GOT TO BE HERE someplace," David muttered as he spread out his copy of the building's blueprints on the worktable he'd set up in the finished basement. The lighting wasn't great, but it was enough to allow him to see the marks he'd made where he'd already checked the structural integrity of the walls. He'd saved the most difficult for last. The east wall was partially blocked by the heating and cooling units and a new hot-water heater.

If there was a hidden room down here, Chesty had camouflaged it well. But then, apparently, the speak-easy that had been located here had been equally discreet; it had never been raided once. During the past week, David had done some digging in the books he owned about the Prohibition era in Chicago and he'd found a few references to Chester "Chesty" Ferguson, but they'd only consisted of a sentence or two, always being overshadowed by the much more famous figure of the time, Al Capone.

David was leaning forward to check the measurements from the blueprints versus the actual dimensions of the east wall, when what sounded like a rioting mob stampeded into the ice-cream parlor above him. It was Sunday. No workmen were scheduled to show up.

Wondering what was going on, David hurried upstairs to check things out. He was greeted with chaos. And in the center of it was Anastasia, issuing orders to her troops.

"Okay, Ryan and Jason will be painting the ceiling in here. Courtney and Heather, check out those wallpaper rolls against the wall. We've got to make the final choice between those two patterns and start putting up the paper on the far wall. Mom and Dad, you come into the kitchen with me to help Claire."

While she was speaking, she was also backing up—until she bumped right into David. "Sorry." Her startled golden eyes gazed at him over her shoulder. Her hair was haphazardly piled on top of her head today. Her T-shirt had kids' handprints on it and her denim shorts had a few jagged tears in some interesting places. "I didn't know you were going to be here today," she said. "I thought you said you were taking the day off."

David couldn't help the inkling of suspicion that crept into his mind. What was she up to? She looked so guilty. Or was it just plain dismayed? She'd been deliberately avoiding him for the past week and he'd missed her. A lot. "What's going on here?" he asked.

"Nothing for you to be worried about. Go back downstairs and do whatever it was you were doing." Putting her hands on his shoulders, she turned him toward the basement door. "Forget all about us."

"Not possible," he assured her wryly.

Anastasia wondered what he meant by that, if not

being able to forget her was a good thing in his book, when she was distracted by her mom.

"Aren't you going to introduce us?" With her salt-and-pepper hair and dainty appearance, Shirley Knight might look like an angelic sweetie, but she had the mind of a steel trap and no man in Anastasia's life had been able to avoid getting caught in her steely snare.

"Sure, Mom, this is David Sullivan, Claire's grandson, but he can't talk now because he's in the middle of an important project downstairs," she said all in one breath.

Never one to beat around the bush, Shirley immediately asked, "Is he married?"

"Mom!"

David liked seeing Anastasia embarrassed. She could tell by the way he was grinning at her, the traitor. She could feel her face turning red. Why, she was actually blushing. She hated this. She was an adult. She could handle this. Heaven knows she should be used to her mom by now. The thing was, she *wasn't* used to David and the way he made her feel.

"I'm not married, Mrs. Knight," David replied.

Shirley positively beamed. "How nice."

Anastasia was relieved when her dad joined them, even if it was only to offer some mocking advice. "Run now, son, while you've still got the chance. I'm Anastasia's father, by the way. The name is Bob Knight."

The sound of a Dean Martin song suddenly filled the air with "Everybody Loves Somebody Sometime."

"Dad, I told you to leave your records at home," Jason said.

"I did," Bob replied. "This is a cassette." He proudly pointed to the boom box in one corner. "The record player is too big to bring on the road. Hey, don't touch that volume control!" He took off to vigorously discuss the matter with his sons, neither of whom shared his love for Dean.

"Now, dear," Shirley admonished her husband, "don't get all riled up. You know how you get." Thankfully she took off after him.

"I probably should have warned you that my family was coming over to help Claire today, but I didn't think you were ready to meet them yet," Anastasia said.

"What makes you say that?"

"The fact that no sane person is ever ready to meet my family," she noted with rueful affection. "Put all together, we can be something of a handful."

"You don't think I can handle things?"

Was it her imagination or had he chosen his words deliberately? There was a wicked light in his eyes that threw her a bit. Was David flirting with her? In front of her family?

When he'd first shown up, her heart had almost stopped. Only because she knew what her mother's reaction would be. It was the same whenever Shirley saw her only daughter with a man under sixty. She hadn't always been that way. Before Jason and Ryan had gotten married, she'd been fairly stable.

Oh, sure, she'd had that one lapse when she'd gotten fed up with Dad and sent him to live with Jason for a few days. But since then, her parents had been more lovey-dovey than ever. The problem was that since Jason's wedding last month, her mom had started getting antsy about Anastasia settling down.

Her brothers, sensing that something was up, were bound to add their own teasing to the mix. Which is why she'd wanted David as far away as possible from her family's antics.

But, perverse as David was, she should have known that just meant he'd want to stay that much more.

"Fine," she said. "Stay if you want to. But don't say I didn't warn you."

"I wouldn't dream of it."

As if to prove her point about her brothers, Jason joined them. "If you put my sister in a snit, you're immediately a friend of mine. I'm Jason Knight."

"The bossy brother," Anastasia added.

"And I'm his wife, Heather Grayson-Knight," said a woman who had come up to stand next to Jason.

"The famous radio host of 'Love on the Rocks,'" Anastasia added.

"I don't listen to much radio," David said apologetically.

"David is a graduate of the University of Fun Deprivation," Anastasia explained. "Unlike my other brother, Ryan, who has a great sense of humor. Just one word of warning, don't drink chocolate milk around him."

"Don't ask," Jason said at David's frown of confusion.

"Hey, I heard that," Ryan said as he joined them.

"That chocolate wallpaper incident happened years ago."

"Some things one never forgets," Anastasia said solemnly.

"Or some people," Ryan added with a fond look at the woman who joined them to put her arm around his waist.

"Ryan is referring to his wife, whom he was stupid enough to let go the first time they were together," Anastasia explained. "But now an older and much wiser Ryan has realized his mistake."

"Ryan never admits to making a mistake. Hi, I'm Courtney. Ryan's better half."

"You've got that right," Ryan agreed.

"Anastasia, I think this is such a neat idea, to open an old-fashioned ice-cream parlor," Heather said. "I plan on mentioning it on the air."

"You see why the two of them get along so well," Jason said.

David nodded in sympathy.

"I think it's a brilliant idea," Courtney agreed.

"Make that the three of them," Jason said.

Looking at the three women, David could see that physically they were very different. Tall and slender, Courtney had long pale blond hair, while Heather was shorter and had shoulder-length auburn hair. In his view, Anastasia was the one who stood out. She was like a force of nature, with her golden eyes and long brown hair, which even now was tumbling down, making him long to reach out and run his fingers through it.

"Yeah, well, I didn't invite you guys over here to shoot the breeze," she was telling her brothers.

"You didn't invite us at all," Ryan said. "You demanded our presence."

"You're my brothers. It's my job to browbeat you."

"I thought that's what we had wives for," Ryan retorted. "Ouch!" This as Courtney socked him. "What did I say?"

"He gives you any trouble, just come to me," Anastasia said. "I know where all his dorky-looking baby pictures are."

"You're in most of them," Ryan remarked.

"I was a beautiful baby. You were the only one always grinning like an idiot."

"And you were the one who punched the minister in the nose during our christening," Ryan said. "You should get our mom to tell you that story, David. She does it so well."

"Forget it." Anastasia grabbed one of the telescoping rollers for ceiling painting and shoved it at Ryan. "Here, time is flying. You'd better get started."

"Why are you putting your family to work?" David asked.

"They wanted to help, despite what Ryan said. I figured we could use the extra hands. I mean, the opening is only two weeks away and there's still a lot to be done. And you've been working so hard that I thought you could use some help."

The truth was, David had gotten a tremendous sense of accomplishment from the renovation work he'd been doing. Since starting it, he found himself actually looking forward to getting up in the morning. He'd forgotten how much he enjoyed working with his hands.

"Are you upset that I asked them to help?" Anastasia said.

"No, not at all. You're right, I could use the help, so thanks."

"*Soitenly,*" she quipped with one of her trademark grins before groaning as the sound of Dean Martin's "Welcome to My World" filled the room, and half the surrounding block. "Dad, you've got that turned up too loud."

"Maybe you should have my grandmother put on her Bruce Springsteen tape," David suggested.

"Oh, so you noticed that, did you?"

"It was hard not to when her musical tastes used to be limited to Lawrence Welk," he noted dryly.

Anastasia shrugged. "All I did was play the tape in my car and she liked it."

"So she told me. She also told me to mind my own business where she and Ira are concerned."

"I told you that, too," Anastasia reminded him.

"Yeah, but I listened to her."

She smiled. "Well, that's a point in your favor."

"So you're not mad at me anymore?"

She eyed him with caution. "This isn't another attempt to get me back in your corner so that you can gang up on Claire?"

"Cross my heart and hope to die," he solemnly vowed.

She remembered how he'd looked at her so apologetically, oozing sex appeal and remorse, once before. But this time there was an earnestness that she decided to trust. "Okay, but you screw up this time and you're in deep doo-doo."

He grinned. "For a librarian, you have such a way with words."

"Must be the Three Stooges' influence on me."

"Anastasia, I'm going to grab your parents for their input in the kitchen," Claire called out.

"Go right ahead." To David, Anastasia added, "My mom is going to help Claire whip up a few batches of ice cream while my dad samples them. Your grandmother is still experimenting with special flavors."

"Yes, I know," he said in amusement. "Avoid the peach-peppermint pecan."

"In the olden days they actually had flavors like asparagus or oyster soup ice cream. Delmonico's in New York had pumpernickel rye bread ice cream on their menu. Compared to that, the peach-peppermint pecan isn't so bad." She knew something else that wasn't so bad, and that was David's smile. That dimple of his flashed and she was a goner.

"I would think that naming the place would be more important than thinking up new flavors of ice cream."

"I heard that," Claire said as she came through the kitchen's swing door with a spoonful of ice cream in hand. "Here, taste this."

David eyed it cautiously. "What is it?"

"Ice cream."

"What flavoooo—" The ending of the word was

cut off by his grandmother sticking the spoon in his mouth.

"It was melting," she explained. "Bob thought it was good, right, Bob?" she turned to ask over her shoulder.

"You bet. I think I'm going to have to loosen my belt a notch or two before I get out of here," Bob said.

Her dad had gained some weight since retiring from the Chicago Transit Authority and his thick hair was now entirely white, but to Anastasia he'd always be the man who righted the world's wrongs when she was little, the one who'd helped give her the confidence to go out and fight her own battles.

"The ice cream is...interesting," David said. "What is it?"

"Cranberry."

David grimaced. "Not my favorite."

"I didn't catch the name of your ice-cream parlor," Bob said to Claire.

"That's because she hasn't settled on one yet," David said.

"How about Cone Home?" Ryan paused in his painting to suggest from the far corner.

"Or The Inside Scoop," Heather suggested from the table where she and Courtney had spread out the wallpaper rolls.

The next suggestion came from Jason, of all people. "Or The Big Dipper."

Claire waved her arms in excitement. "That's it! That's the name. I knew I'd know the right one as soon as I heard it."

"And not a moment too soon," David noted. "The grand opening is only two weeks away."

"I'll call the sign maker right away and tell him to go ahead with that design I chose. The Big Dipper," Claire repeated. "Yes, it feels right."

BY THE TIME her family left, it was nearly dark. "I can't thank you enough for having everyone come over and help out the way they did," Claire said.

"That's what friends and their family are for."

"Friends don't come better than you." Claire gave her a big hug. "The Big Dipper has its name and its wallpaper thanks to the Knight family. I know that most of the walls are painted blue, but that one far wall really needed something to make it stand out and I think we've got it."

The wallpaper pattern was cheerful and old-fashioned at the same time, and had been the unanimous nomination of both Heather and Courtney.

"Where's David?" Claire asked.

"He went downstairs about an hour ago," Anastasia replied, relieved that David had escaped round two of her mother's inquisition.

Claire shook her head and clucked with matronly concern. "The poor boy never rests."

"When I asked him once what he believes in, he said hard work and baseball. Not dreams. He told me that his dad risked everything for some foolish idea and that the rest of the family had to pay for that."

"Oh, my!" Claire put her hand to her mouth, her eyes reflecting her concern. "I had no idea he felt that way. It's true that my son was a dreamer and he didn't plan his finances very well, but he had no way of knowing his life and his wife's would be cut short in a head-on collision. The accident wasn't his fault.''

"Does David know that?" Anastasia gently asked.

"Yes, I've told him many times, but he can be stubborn when he gets an idea into his head.''

"No kidding." Her voice was rueful. "He told me that there weren't many arson investigators who were dreamers. I'm thinking that maybe that's what appealed to him about the job.''

"You could be right. I keep hoping this leave of absence will be good for him, give him some time off, but he's not getting much rest when he works all day up here and then goes to the basement.''

"Doing more repairs?"

"No, he's mostly puttering down there.''

"I've never seen him puttering," Anastasia mused. It sounded as if David had discovered something that had captured his attention. Being the imaginative type herself, she immediately began wondering what it could be. "Let's go take a look.''

They found him in a far corner of the basement, rapping his knuckles on the wall and acting most suspiciously. But there was an excitement about him that was unmistakable. This wasn't a man interested in making repairs, this was a guy with a mission—and missions weren't all that far from dreams.

"Is this your version of puttering and, if so, can anyone play?" Anastasia cheerfully inquired.

8

DAVID JUMPED a foot before turning to face them.

"Oh-ho," Anastasia teased him. "Get a load of that guilty look on his face, Claire. I think we caught him searching for hidden treasure down here."

"He always did love a treasure hunt when he was a young boy," Claire said fondly.

"Really? I would never have guessed that. So what kind of treasure are you looking for, David?" Anastasia asked as she walked over to the blueprints.

"I'm not looking for treasure."

"You should be," Claire said. "This building has a colorful history."

He looked at his grandmother with surprise. "You know about that?"

"Just that there were rumors that the place had once been used as a speakeasy."

"No kidding!" Anastasia was impressed. "Why didn't you tell me?"

"Because she didn't want you knocking out the walls looking for hidden rooms," David replied.

Anastasia frowned. "Why would I do that?"

"So *that's* what you've been doing down here in the basement," Claire said with a slow smile.

Anastasia glanced from David to Claire. "What do you mean?"

"David has found something," Claire replied.

"He has?"

Claire nodded before turning to her grandson. "Tell her."

"It's no big deal," David maintained. "All I found was a three-foot discrepancy between the measurements in the blueprints and the actual measurements of the walls down here. It could and most likely *is* just a simple error."

"Then why were you knocking on the walls?" Anastasia asked.

"Because he was looking for a secret storage room," Claire replied on his behalf.

"Maybe I was looking for termites," David retorted.

"The building is brick," Claire said, "and we already had that pest control company give it a clean bill of health."

"Okay, so I was looking for a storage room of some kind."

"You don't have to make it sound as if you'd committed some awful crime you feel terrible about," Anastasia gently chastised him. "This is exciting. This is cool. This is—"

"Probably nothing," he interjected, trying to be practical. "Look what happened when Geraldo Rivera had that disastrous special where he opened Al Capone's safe on live TV. There was nothing of value inside."

But even as David spoke, Anastasia could see the

light in his eyes and she knew that whether he wanted to admit it or not, he was hooked on following what amounted to a treasure-hunting dream.

She couldn't help herself. Going over to him, she gave him a big bear hug and whispered, "I'm so proud of you."

He looked down at her with typical male confusion at her unexpected action before adding a typical, for him, word of caution. "There's no sense getting your hopes up."

She grinned at him. "Ah, but then I've never been known to be sensible."

She couldn't be sure, but she could have sworn that he murmured, "Thank heaven for that."

"HE'S STARTING TO BEND." Betty was practically smacking her lips with satisfaction. "I told you that adding the temptation of a secret room would get him on the road to believing in dreams."

"I still fail to see the connection," Hattie said from atop the intricately carved post on the mirrored back bar behind the counter.

"He's on a treasure hunt," Betty explained. "Just like he was when he was a kid."

Hattie frowned. "But we're supposed to be working on uniting Anastasia with her soul mate, that's our job. Not making David believe in dreams."

"To do one we have to do the other."

"This is getting complicated." Hattie rubbed her forehead with her magic wand as she muttered, "You know how I feel about complicated. I don't like it."

"You don't like khaki, either," Muriel said, "but

that doesn't change the reality of life. And the reality is that we need David to believe in dreams before he and Anastasia can have a happily-ever-after.''

"I'll bet guardian angels don't have to deal with things like this," Hattie grumbled. "I'll bet they have easier lives than we do. They have to, with those gorgeous elegant wings they have. Not these little stubby ones like we're stuck with."

"I've told you before, your wings are just as aerodynamically sound as a guardian angel's are," Muriel retorted. "Besides, you have nothing to complain about. You're not the one with an ear infection that makes flying difficult. I keep losing my equilibrium."

Hattie waved her wand in the air as an idea struck her. "I'll bet that's what happened when I accidentally spilled too much intelligence-and-attitude fairy dust on Anastasia. I'll bet I had an ear infection and never knew it."

"Nice try, but you spilled it because you were showing off, as usual. As I recall, you were practicing fairy dust with a flourish, going on about how presentation is everything, and flaunting that showy velvet pillow you've got..."

"It's not showy!" Hattie protested. "It's royal purple velvet draped with elegant folds of sheer chiffon shot through with strands of gold and purple threads. Nestled in the midst of all that splendor is a glorious gilded vessel adorned with cherubs."

"Right," Muriel scoffed. "Like I said. Showy. And it wasn't your equilibrium that was off, it was the pillow's. You couldn't resist giving us one of your triumphantly superior looks, and the break in your concentration was enough for the pillow to tilt and spill the fairy dust.''

"Oh, horsefeathers!" Hattie exclaimed. "As if you'd remember details like that thirty-three years later."

Muriel shrugged. "That's only a blink of an eye in fairy-godmother time."

"Enough, you two," Betty growled. "If we could return to the subject of Anastasia and David? Now, as I've said, I think Claire has been tremendously useful in keeping things moving along. You saw how Anastasia's face softened when Claire said that David had hunted treasure as a kid?"

Hattie and Muriel nodded.

"Good. Then we continue with our plan, keeping in mind that timing is everything. If David discovers that room too soon, it won't have the effect we want. Ditto if it's too late. Understand?"

Hattie raised her hand. "Um, how do we know when the time is right?"

"It's your job to know."

"It's my job to do a lot of things I can't do," Hattie muttered.

"Your magic wand will glow when the time is right," Betty said.

"Provided she can see it," Muriel interjected. "Remember, she's the one who wouldn't wear her glasses and hence got us in the wrong line in heaven."

Hattie glared at Muriel. "I don't appreciate that comment. As if you could have done any better."

"I could have."

"But you didn't, so put a sock in it!" Hattie flew

down to join Muriel on the white marble counter, pulling up the sleeves on her golden chiffon gown as if preparing for a fisticuffs. "I've had enough of your harping on this! So back off!"

To Hattie's astonishment, Muriel grinned at her and gave her a big hug of approval. "That's better! You've learned how to stand up for yourself and fight like a fairy godmother. Good for you. Now I know you're my sister."

"Mine, too," Betty said with approval, joining them in a group hug.

"Watch my hat." Hattie clasped it to her silvery curls with one hand as she returned their sisterly embrace with the other, before adding, "And while you're feeling so jolly, why don't you just let me do a bit of redecorating in here? They don't have the color scheme right yet. All this red, white and blue. I feel like I'm in a production of *Damn Yankees*. They need more lavender and pink."

With a whisk of her magic wand, Hattie transformed the walls into lavender and pink stripes.

"Forget it," Betty said, returning the room to its former colors. "You're a fairy godmother, for petunia's sake, not Martha Stewart. Save your magic for the big stuff."

"DO YOU UNDERSTAND where I'm coming from?" Anastasia was sitting in the softer of her two cozy chintz chairs, her cat curled up on her lap and gazing up at her with blue eyes. "It's not that I'm taking the mouse's side over yours. My brother had a pet mouse so I can't just kill this mouse that's bothering you.

And, okay, I admit my reluctance might also have something to do with the Miss Mouse puppet I sometimes use at storytime at work. Heck, for all I know, it could have started the first time I ever saw Mickey Mouse. Just like reading *Charlotte's Web* traumatized me about killing spiders, I now have this thing against hurting mice."

She paused to rub Xena's ears the way the feline loved before continuing. "Don't get me wrong, I don't want him living here any more than you do. And I can't believe he had the nerve to show up again. But I've reset the trap. The next time I catch him, I'm taking him for a long ride. Well, not too long, he gets all hyper when he's confined and I don't want him to hurt himself."

The cat purred.

It was all the encouragement Anastasia needed to go on. "And it's not as if you're the only one upset around here. Put yourself in my shoes. David is driving me crazy. One minute I think he's impossible, then I think he's got potential, then I think he's adorable and sexy as all get out. What's wrong with me?"

Anastasia looked around her living room as if she could find the answer there. She'd deliberately left this room mostly empty, allowing the few pieces to speak for themselves. The colorful Moroccan table should have clashed with the chintz-covered chairs, each with a different floral pattern, but it didn't. The same way that the "Silence Is Golden" Balinese wood carving of a mask with a finger to its lips complemented rather than distracted from the posters and framed prints of her favorite children's-book illustrators, from Susan Jeffers to old-fashioned classics by Jessie Wilcox Smith, that also adorned the walls.

Finding no answer in her surroundings, she resumed her monologue with Xena. "You know that David kissed me and then left me hanging. Of course, that night he took me to Rosa's I did kiss him and leave him hanging. So I guess we're even now. But I have this feeling that it's going to be up to me to make the next move. I should just do it, right? Not sit here talking to you about it. Okay." She reached for the phone. "I'm calling him now."

She'd gotten David's phone number the morning after his jumping jacks had woken her up before dawn. "Are you busy?" she asked, barely giving him time to say hello.

"Depends why you're asking," he cautiously replied.

Her voice was husky with promise as she said, "Meet me downstairs in the ice-cream parlor in half an hour and you'll find out."

SHE MET HIM even sooner than that, running into him on the stairs leading downstairs. She'd changed from the cutoffs and T-shirt she'd worn earlier in the day into a comfortable amber-colored rayon challis dress that flowed around her legs as she walked. Her buttery soft sandals made tiny clicking sounds on the steps as she tried to regain her balance.

His arms came around her to steady her. She felt warm and protected until he used his high-handed voice on her. "You move too fast."

"You have this tendency to be bossy, have you

noticed?'' she asked as she stepped away to unlock the door to The Big Dipper with the key Claire had given her. David had a similar key, but she'd gotten to the door first.

"Me?" he said in disbelief, following her inside. "You should talk. You're the one who likes ordering people around."

"I do not."

"What about when your brothers were here earlier?"

"Brothers don't count," she replied, flicking a switch that turned on the Tiffany-style lamps on either side of the mirrored back bar, illuminating the area with a warm glow. "And I'll have you know that they've ordered me around plenty. Especially Jason. And that made me determined to grow up and not have anyone tell me what to do. You can't imagine what it's like growing up with bossy brothers."

"No, I can't."

His words made her realize he'd grown up without any siblings and without his parents. "I'm sorry. I guess your childhood was very different from mine."

He shrugged. "I was lucky to have such wonderful grandparents. My grandfather died a few days after I graduated from college. His heart gave out. I never even knew that he'd been a soda jerk or that he and my grandmother met in an ice-cream parlor. You knew before I did."

She sensed that was a sore point with him. Wanting to cheer him up, she grinned and said, "Yeah, well, sometimes I'm nosy that way."

"You take the time to listen."

"I can teach you how to do that. Starting tonight. It all starts with ice cream and imagination. The only caveat is that you have to keep your hands at your sides at all times. Think you can manage that? This will be a test of your willpower."

"I'm known for my willpower," he bragged.

"That's what I figured. So something like this—" she leaned forward to place a string of tiny kisses along his chin "—wouldn't bother you in the least, right?"

"Right." His resonant voice was even gruffer than usual, and sexier.

Anastasia smiled with anticipation. She was looking forward to this. He might have said on the stairway that she moved too fast, but she didn't think he'd complain about her boldness tonight.

"So what's the big surprise?" he demanded.

"Come behind the counter and you'll see. Well, actually, you might not *see*, because I'll have to blindfold you for this next segment."

"Will this procedure involve silk sheets and handcuffs?" He made the question sound hopeful.

"No. Why? Were you counting on that?"

"Maybe."

"Too bad. You'll have to use your imagination instead." Leaning closer, she arranged the black silk scarf she'd just undone from around her own throat so that it covered his eyes. "No peeking," she warned him.

"You're not going to be doing anything that passersby shouldn't be seeing, are you?" he asked with equal parts of anticipation and concern.

"Like stripping naked, you mean?"

"Yeah, that would qualify," he noted dryly.

"Of course not."

"Too bad."

She laughed. "Okay, let's get started with a little biology lesson."

"That sounds promising."

"Did you know that your tongue is the home for nine thousand taste buds and that each little taste bud has ten to fifteen receptors that tell the brain if something you're tasting is salty, sour or sweet?"

David shook his head. All he knew was that talking about tongues got him thinking wicked thoughts about licking melting ice cream from her naked body. That was probably her plan. To drive him crazy. Well, two could play that game.

Blindly reaching out, he got lucky and captured her hand. Lifting it to his mouth, he licked the sensitive skin between her thumb and index fingers. "Mmm, sweet and salty. All nine thousand taste buds agree."

Relying on his sense of touch, he uncurled her fingers until he found her palm. He swirled his tongue in a seductive pattern intended to melt her kneecaps.

She had to clear her throat twice before she could speak. "Are you ready to sample some of the goodies?"

"More than ready." His voice was husky.

"Open up."

He parted his lips, ready to consume her mouth in a kiss hot enough to peel paint. Instead, she slipped a tiny plastic scoop of something cold and tasty in his mouth.

"No one knows for certain where or when ice cream was first created," she said, "but there are lots of colorful stories about its origins. In the first century, it's said that Emperor Nero was so addicted that he sent runners to the Alps for snow."

David was beginning to understand the concept of addiction. He was becoming addicted to the sexy sound of her voice. That storyteller, Scheherazade, must have had a voice like Anastasia's.

"It took a month to bring the snow back to Rome where Nero would eat it flavored with fruit juices or honey. What you're sampling now is a cherry sorbet."

The cherry taste and image made him think of her lips and how they'd taste after the cold sorbet. Before he could find out, she'd put another tiny sample in his mouth.

"Legend has it that Marco Polo came back from his journeys in China with a recipe for frozen cream. It became known as *gelati*, iced cream. What you're sampling now is a rich French vanilla. When Catherine de Médicis moved to France to marry the king, she brought along her chef who knew how to make *gelati* and the French were exposed to the delights."

David could swear she was using these words deliberately. Exposed. Delights. He was getting all hot and bothered thinking about her body, not blasted ice cream.

"Are you still listening?" she asked. "After all, this is supposed to be an exercise in listening and focusing on your senses."

"Oh, I'm focusing, all right," he said hoarsely. He didn't tell her on what.

"In the 1600s Charles the First of England hired a French chef who brought the recipe for ice cream with him. The English king paid the chef to keep the recipe a royal secret, but once the king was beheaded, the secret of ice-cream making spread around the world. George Washington ate it, spending two hundred dollars on ice cream in one summer. That was a small fortune in those days. But the taste is so sinfully delicious, who can resist it?" She slipped another sample in his mouth.

Sinful, most definitely. The ice cream was good but she was better, building things up the way you built a good fire. With enough embers beneath it to sustain the flames.

"Americans created ice-cream cones and ice-cream sodas. And then there's the ice-cream sundae, which legend has it was developed right here in Evanston, sometimes called 'Heavenston' because of its strict observance of the Sabbath. Men who worked on Sunday would receive a written rebuke in the local newspaper. Selling ice-cream sodas on Sundays was looked upon as a wicked distraction and was outlawed."

David's thoughts should be outlawed. And talk about wicked! As for a distraction, he'd never met a distraction like Anastasia.

"To get around the law, on Sundays, ice-cream parlors and soda fountains served ice cream with just the syrup and no soda. The combination of cold ice cream and warmed chocolate syrup can be irresistible.

Mmm." She fed him a spoonful. "An incredible combination."

"I know an even better combination," he growled, his willpower reduced to red-hot embers as he took hold of the hand that fed him and tugged her into his arms. Instinct and need guided his mouth to hers as he kissed her blindly, hotly, tenderly.

As his lips consumed hers, Anastasia decided that he tasted better than any ice cream on the planet.

Sliding the blindfold from his eyes, she saw the passion in their blue depths before her own lids fluttered shut, allowing her to focus on what she could feel. He teased her lips with his tongue, coaxing her to part them and rewarding her when she did.

She could taste the chocolate and the incredible essence that was pure David.

One kiss merged into the next as passion flared out of control. Somehow they ended up on the padded bench near the back of the ice-cream parlor. His provocative fingers slid over her thigh, her rayon dress amplifying his touch.

A trail of heated kisses from the corner of her mouth to the hollow of her collarbone ended at the neckline of her dress. With each button on her dress that he unfastened, he paused to celebrate by returning his mouth to hers for a mind-blowing tangle of nibbles and delicate tongue thrusts before beginning another trail of kisses and undoing yet another button.

It took her a moment or two to think clearly enough to reciprocate by unbuttoning his shirt, and her fingers lacked the nimble talent of his, but what she lacked in finesse she made up for in enthusiasm. The first touch of his bare chest beneath her palm made her pause to enjoy the freedom to touch him.

When he slid his hand beneath her silky chemise to reverently cup her bare breast, she couldn't prevent her gasp of sheer pleasure. Incorporating it into their kiss, he shifted it from blind hunger to a new plateau of erotic anticipation.

He moved slower now, as if he had all the time in the world to enjoy the wonders of her body. And he was touching her and kissing her as if she was a wonder, as if he was intrigued and delighted with everything about her.

Reclining on the bench, she paid no heed to the hard wood beneath her, only to the hard body above her. She could feel the muscles of his thighs flexing against her own as he used his weight to create an intimate, electric connection that brought in a new dimension of desire. His touch inflamed her, as hers seemed to inflame him.

The thud of his heart mirrored the uneven beating of her own. There was something wickedly sensual about his hand being beneath her silk chemise, caressing the soft swell of her breast, more so than if she'd been completely bare before him. She couldn't see what his hand was doing, she could only feel it. And feel it she did, right down to the center of her womb. Brushing the ball of his thumb against her tingling nipples created a bliss so powerful it was almost painful.

As if sensing that, he lowered his mouth to the sensitive flesh and kissed her through the silk, feathering the crest with the tip of his tongue.

Weaving her fingers through his dark hair, she clung to him as passion pulsed through her lower body. When his mouth finally returned to hers, their kiss took on a new intensity and fire.

She wanted more. She wanted no clothing between them. He wanted the same thing. He told her so with every thrust of his tongue, with every shift of his hips. He was about to peel her dress from her shoulders when light exploded all around them.

Swearing under his breath, David sat upright, shielding her with his body. "What the hell…"

"Oh my!" Claire gasped, her eyes as big as saucers.

9

"I DIDN'T MEAN to interrupt," Claire said in an embarrassed voice. "I didn't know anyone would be here this late. I saw the lights were on, I thought maybe I left them on, but I thought I had turned them off, but maybe I should have known that it was you two, not that I could guess, I mean, it's none of my business... I'm babbling."

"It's not a problem," Anastasia hastily assured Claire despite the fact that her heart was pounding a mile a minute as she hastily rebuttoned her dress. "This is your business. I mean The Big Dipper is your place of business and you have the right to walk in anytime you choose, and besides how could you have known... Now I'm babbling. David, say something." Her voice reflected her desperation.

His voice, drat his hide, was amused. "Why should I? I'm having too much fun watching you two stumble around. Besides, I don't do babble."

"Do you want to hit him, Claire, or should I?" Anastasia asked.

"What?" David demanded. "What did I say?"

"Well, dear, you do have a way of putting your foot in your mouth. But I love you anyway." Claire patted his arm reassuringly.

"What made you come back to The Big Dipper tonight?" David asked her. "I thought you were tired and were going to make an early night of it."

"I did try, but I woke up after having the strangest dream about a fairy godmother who wore wild hats." Claire shook her head in puzzlement. "Anyway, then I got to worrying about the grand opening so I decided to come over and check out a few things in the kitchen. I never dreamed I'd walk in on the two of you..."

Anastasia could feel herself blushing again, for only the second time this year—and David was responsible both times. She had to get out of here before she made a fool of herself, or rather a *bigger* fool.

Because it was finally sinking in that she was falling in love with David and she still had some serious doubts about the wisdom of such a move. Fooling around, having fun, was one thing. But loving someone like David, so unlike the usual guys she went for, could be very risky. Time to regroup here.

"Yes, well, I'd better get back upstairs," Anastasia hurriedly said. "David can stay down here and help you do...whatever it is you need to do to get ready for the opening. I mean, I do have to go to work tomorrow. A full day. I've got to practice a new finger-play routine, and I've got a class of first-graders coming in for a tour of the library, plus I've got that Gaylord sales rep coming by in the afternoon. I'm babbling again. I never babble. I'm going now."

"There's no need, dear," Claire began, but Anastasia had already fled.

"WHAT'S THE POINT of having a beeper if you're not going to answer your page?" Betty demanded of Hattie, who was ten seconds late for the emergency meeting Betty had just called in Anastasia's living room.

"Is that why my magic wand was blinking?" Hattie held it up to the light to study it. "At first I thought it was glowing because the time had come for David to find the secret room, then I remembered you said the wand would glow not blink. Then I thought perhaps it needed new batteries or something."

"They don't need batteries, they're solar powered, you should know that by now," Muriel informed her, but Hattie was already distracted by a stack of illustrations that Anastasia had been working on in her apartment.

Her voice warm with fondness, Hattie said, "Remember when Anastasia was a little girl, and it was almost as if she could actually see and hear us?"

Betty nodded. "I'm sure that's why she tells such wonderful fairy-godmother stories."

"I must say, however, that I'm much prettier than Anastasia is drawing me. And she has me wearing green." Hattie slowly shook her head. "I rarely wear green. It makes my complexion look sallow."

"Oh, give it a break, would you?" Muriel exclaimed. "We've got bigger problems to deal with here."

Hattie blinked ingenuously. "What problems? Where is Anastasia?"

"Asleep in the other room."

"Then what's the problem? Why call this emergency meeting? I'd say she and David were getting along quite well. As for Claire walking in on them in a most inopportune moment, well, that's Betty's fault.''

Betty seemed surprised by this news. ''How do you figure that?''

''You were the one who wanted to enlist a human's help,'' Hattie reminded her.

Betty defended her actions. ''All I did was put the idea of David and Anastasia as a couple into Claire's head.''

''Then you should have put it into her head to stay home tonight,'' Hattie told her.

Betty was not amused by the reprimand. ''Hey, accidents happen. And what was that about Claire having a dream about a fairy godmother wearing wild hats? Did you have something to do with that, Hattie?''

''I most certainly did not,'' she replied haughtily. ''I don't own any *wild* hats. What are you two laughing at?''

Betty and Muriel pointed to the haberdashery confection Hattie had atop her head at that very moment, a lavish affair decorated with plenty of orange and yellow mums along with a chirping yellow parakeet.

''Do you think the bow is a bit much?'' she asked, indicating the golden ribbon tied under her chin.

Her question made her sisters laugh even harder, until they were doing tumbling somersaults in midair, so intense was their mirth.

''Well, fiddlesticks!'' Hattie stomped her foot on the back of the chintz chair she was standing on, nearly losing her gilded pumps in the process. ''I'm certainly not going to stick around here and be laughed at. Anastasia is *my* charge and *I* say she's doing just fine.''

As she disappeared in a purple puff of displeasure, Muriel wryly noted to Betty, ''The problem is that she also says she doesn't own any wild hats. So what does that tell us about her judgment?''

Betty sighed. ''That we're not out of the woods yet. How many days left until our retirement?''

''Too many,'' was Muriel's glum reply.

ANASTASIA SPENT her Monday too busy with work to worry about David. But the moment she got in her car to drive home, he was center stage in her mind once again. Rather than running from the thought of loving him, she decided to take it out and examine it.

What would be so bad about loving him? Other than the fact that he had a tendency to be impossibly bossy and controlling, not to mention highly suspicious of others. The only interest she shared with him was an appreciation of the Three Stooges and a love for Claire. Without a doubt, he was vastly different from any of the men she'd fallen for in the past—not that there had been hoards of them.

Now for the positive column. The way he made her feel. The way he smiled as if he'd almost forgotten how. The way he had her and Claire's best interests at heart even if he was being a pain about responsibility and reality. The way he'd undertaken the treasure hunt. The fact that underneath all that bluster he was a good man who probably was as confused about this relationship as she was.

While she might be falling in love with him, that was no reason to think that he was falling for her. Okay, so he showed signs of being attracted. And he kissed her as if he meant it.

But he still hadn't given her any verbal indication of his feelings. *Smoky looks hot enough to melt steel* didn't count. That could just be lust speaking.

The moment she entered her apartment, her worries about David had to take a back seat to the realization that the mouse was back in its trap. She'd been trying to catch him for days. The peanut-butter bait had finally done the trick.

Keeping her car keys in one hand, she used an oven mitt to carry the trap, not because it was hot, but because the last time she'd carried the trap outside she could feel the mouse's movements inside and it had freaked her a bit. Hurrying downstairs, she raced toward her car. She was just about ready to drive away when David suddenly appeared from inside The Big Dipper.

"We need to talk," he said in a no-nonsense tone of voice.

"Get in." She didn't have time to explain that she had to drive the mouse to its new home in the park and that she had to do it quickly so that it didn't get a concussion or something from banging its head against the sides of the trap. Thinking the mouse might feel more secure if it couldn't see where it was going, she'd covered it as best she could with the oven mitt.

"Your oven mitt is moving," David noted as they zoomed away from the curb.

"That's because there's a mouse in it."

His strangled exclamation was not a pretty thing.

"Relax," she reassured him, taking one hand off the wheel to pat his denim-clad leg. "The mouse is in its trap."

Putting her hand back on the steering wheel, David didn't know which scared him more—the mouse or Anastasia's wild driving.

"And the reason we're taking the mouse for a drive is?" he asked, sarcasm masking his discomfort. "He's bored with our neighborhood or what?"

"He keeps coming back."

"How do you know it's even the same mouse?"

"I just know," she said, changing gears to stop at a red light.

"You could have a dozen mice in your apartment."

"Listen, if I had a dozen mice, Xena would not be sleeping at night. And neither would I. No, it's the same mouse. I can tell. He's laughing at me. And he's taunting Xena."

"Then exterminate him."

"I can't do that…"

"Because of Pescado. Right. So where are you taking Mr. Mouse?"

"To that park near Northwestern," she replied, shifting into first as the light turned green.

"So it can go terrorize some poor gorgeous coed in her dorm room?"

She frowned. That hadn't occurred to her. "Do you have a better idea? Other than extermination?"

"No," he had to admit.

"Fine." She decided the gorgeous coeds were on their own. "Then it's the park."

"Providing we live long enough to get there," he muttered, grabbing the door handle as she zipped around an illegally parked car to take a corner.

"Calm down. I'm a good driver. So what did you want to talk about?"

David hadn't expected to have this discussion with a trapped mouse six inches away from him. His voice was curt as he said, "About what happened the other night."

"Yes?"

"I didn't plan that."

"I know. Neither did I. When I invited you downstairs, I thought we might get closer, but I had no way of knowing that things would get so...so intense and out of hand so quickly. I wasn't trying to be a tease or anything like that." She shifted the Triumph to a lower gear as she rounded yet another corner before stealing a look at David.

Could one nervous blue-eyed look from him be the deciding factor? Could it push her over the edge and make falling in love with him a done deal? Granted, David's look *had* been directed at the captive mouse, but she'd felt the strangest tug at her heartstrings and the strongest sense of recognition. Which sounded more like something from one of the fairy tales she read the kids than real life.

She didn't have time to dwell on her thoughts because she had to move fast to get the last parking space near the park. As the red Triumph jerked to a halt, she heard David heave a sigh of relief.

It was short-lived as the mouse wiggled, scooting the trap out from under the oven mitt and almost into David's lap. Leaping up like a man in the hot seat, he scrambled out of the car with more speed than dignity.

"You don't like mice," Anastasia noted.

"I don't know many people who do, besides you."

"Like I told Xena, it's not that I like the mouse personally, it's just that I—"

"Don't want it killed. I know." David stuffed his hands into his back jean pockets, as if to get them as far away as possible from the rodent. "So get a move on and let him go. For all we know there could be a city ordinance against releasing mice in a city park."

"I certainly hope not."

As she carried the mousetrap from the car, she couldn't help appreciating the beauty of the park, located on Lake Michigan. The sky was overcast, looking as if it couldn't make up its mind whether to rain or not. But that only made the gunmetal blues and greens of the lake more vibrant. One or two trees in the park were starting to change into their fall colors. She knew from experience that, come October, the maples and oaks would be brilliant.

But for now she had to focus her attention on the mouse, which once she'd brought to the middle of the park was showing a marked reluctance to leave the trap even though she'd unlatched the opening.

"Just shake him out," David ordered impatiently.

She did, a little too forcefully. The mouse flew into the air and almost landed on David's shoulder. A diving movement was all that saved David. It didn't save

Anastasia, whom he rammed into before knocking them both to the ground. By rolling at the last minute, he was able to cushion her from the worst of the fall with his body.

It happened so fast that Anastasia couldn't quite believe that she was actually lying plastered against David's chest while he groaned beneath her. Feeling guilty that she'd put on a few pounds since sampling Claire's ice-cream flavors, she hurriedly rolled off him.

"Are you okay?" she asked, putting her head down to listen to his heart beat just for the sheer pleasure of it, not out of any lifesaving techniques.

He nodded, but she couldn't see him. So he lifted her head, threading his fingers through her gorgeous long hair. It was like silk. And she smelled incredible.

The long brown skirt she'd been wearing was hiked up, displaying a tantalizing glimpse of her calves. Her orange top and brown suede vest made her look adorable, while the silk scarf she wore was tied in a jaunty knot at the base of her throat.

He drew her closer, using his hands to guide her to him until her mouth rested upon his so that he could delicately sip at her parted lips as if she were a rare wine. Not that he was a wine kind of guy, but damn, she was intoxicating. Kissing her packed more of a punch than a bottle of Jack Daniel's.

It was his last thought before he became lost in the intimacies of her tongue tangling with his. When her thigh slid between his legs, he trapped it there, his hands on her back pressing her closer to his fully aroused body.

"Hey, you two!" a male voice shouted. "No making out in the park."

David winced as Anastasia scrambled off his painfully hard body. Damn, she'd be the death of him yet!

"It's the police," she whispered in a scandalized voice.

"You heard me, you two. Take it someplace else." As the officer got closer, he said, "Geez, you're both old enough to know better." Pausing a moment, he said, "Hey, Sullivan, is that you?"

David groaned. Out of all the officers in all the suburbs, he had to be stopped by Abe Carver, who'd attended the same arson investigation conference that David had back in August—before Anastasia had knocked him off his feet, literally and figuratively.

"Hey, man, I heard you were on a leave of absence, but I had no idea it was so you could make out in the park," Abe said, pounding David on the back with a macho enthusiasm shared by sports figures and cops. "Must be a tough life."

"Right," David replied through gritted teeth and a false smile. "We were just leaving."

"I'll have you know that I never blushed until I met you," Anastasia had the nerve to tell him once they were back in the Triumph.

"You? What about me?"

"You were blushing?" She eyed him carefully as if looking for any remaining signs.

"I'm not the type to get caught necking in a public park," he loftily informed her.

"Meaning, I am? Listen—" turning in her seat, she

jabbed her index finger in his chest "—I may be unconventional about some things, but I..."

"But you what?"

"I like the way you kiss." Her right hand flew to her mouth as if to stop the words from coming out, but it was too late. Ruefully she added, "I wasn't going to say that. It just slipped out. Forget it."

As if forgetting one solitary thing about Anastasia was even remotely possible. David sincerely doubted that it was.

THE FEW REMAINING days before The Big Dipper's grand opening raced by in a flurry of activity, which was topped off by Ira giving Claire three dozen yellow roses and a kiss at the ribbon-cutting ceremony as the ice-cream parlor officially opened for business. The four-day-long celebration was a successful one, thanks in part to Heather mentioning The Big Dipper on her radio talk show. A number of customers who came in said they were fans of "Love on the Rocks: Where Relationships are Stirred Not Shaken."

As a show of appreciation, Claire renamed the Rainforest Brittle ice cream Love on the Rocks in Heather's honor. It immediately sold out.

Saturday, things got so busy that David was drafted into working behind the counter as customers continued to flock in. He'd started out bussing tables but got roped into counter duty by Anastasia, who replaced him with Barry, the student help Claire had hired only the day before.

"Why can't Barry work up front?" David said

even as Anastasia was dragging him behind the counter.

"Because Claire hasn't finished training him yet."

"She didn't train me, either."

"I gave you a crash course in ice-cream history and this is the way you treat me?"

"Well, if you put it like that. I wouldn't want you to think I was unappreciative of that unforgettable lesson or anything." Giving her a wolfish smile that took her breath away, he swaggered over to the next customer in line and took their order.

By the end of the business day, David was showing some of his grandfather's flare for the dramatic by actually completing a one-handed toss of a scoop of butter pecan. The bad news was that he missed the tulip sundae dish he was aiming for. The good news was that he also narrowly missed hitting Anastasia with the ice cream he'd launched. Instead, it landed with a plop on the tile floor.

While cleaning it up, David realized that he'd actually had a great time, which was weird because he'd always considered himself to be a high-intensity macho kind of guy and an ice-cream parlor wasn't exactly a den of masculinity.

He suspected Anastasia would be pleased to know that he was enjoying himself. She was wearing a white bib apron to protect her clothing, as they all were. But she looked particularly good in hers.

"Are you having fun yet?" she teasingly asked him, as she'd often done in the past.

This time, he could say with complete honesty,

"Yeah, I am." He just wasn't sure, yet, how happy he was about that.

DESPITE THE LONG HOURS he'd worked at The Big Dipper on Saturday, David went downstairs to resume what his grandmother and Anastasia had come to refer to as his treasure hunt. He'd pretty much given up on finding anything, but he was nothing if not thorough and there was only a small space left that he had yet to explore.

"David, are you down there?" Anastasia called down, taking a few steps downstairs to confirm that he was.

He paused in his search long enough to appreciate the fact that she'd changed from the jeans and Big Dipper T-shirt working uniform that he still wore, into the incredible dress she'd had on when she'd given him that memorable lesson in ice-cream history and seduction.

"Any luck with the treasure hunt?" Her smile was brighter than the fluorescent lighting.

"I give up. There's nothing down here," he told himself as much as her.

Moving to his side, she gave his arm a reassuring squeeze as she said, "Yes, there is. I can feel it."

"Then lead me to it."

"I wish I could, but I'm not one of those divining rods that can find water holes—or hidden treasures, for that matter." She looked at the blueprints for a moment and then pointed something out. "Wait a minute. See here how the corner isn't quite the way it is in reality? This shows it as a right angle where actually it's more on a slant. Gives you more room that way.''

"That's why they did it that way."

"But it could also be a way of putting a fake front on a corner storage area."

Studying the blueprints again, he said, "You may have a point." Going to the corner, he studied it closely before shaking his head. "I've already examined the area. I'm telling you, there's nothing here." He pushed on the concrete foundation wall to prove his point. To his astonishment a section of the adjoining plastered wall abruptly gave way, popping outward instead of inward.

Anastasia grinned at his awed expression and said just one word. "Bingo."

10

"WHAT'S INSIDE?" Anastasia demanded, her voice trembling with excitement. "Can you see?"

"Not with you blinding me by aiming the flashlight in my eyes," David grumbled.

"Sorry." She adjusted the high-powered beam while trying to peer over his shoulder. "Is that better? It sure is dusty in there," she added, right before sneezing. "Who'd have thought that Chesty was smart enough to have a trick door built into the wall. You know, it sort of looks like a miniature wine cellar."

"I don't understand it," David was muttering. "I checked every inch of this wall before and found absolutely nothing."

"So what's in there?" Her voice was breathless.

His was not. "The shelves are empty," he said. "I told you that would be the case. Just like Geraldo Rivera and Al Capone's empty safe."

"Yes, but in that case, someone from the IRS was standing right beside Geraldo, ready to confiscate anything of value they might find against the umpteen thousand dollars in back taxes Al still owed."

"Yeah, well, that proves that nothing is certain except death and taxes," he drawled.

Anastasia wasn't as willing to give up yet. "Wait a second. I think there's something on the top shelf way in the back. See?" She aimed the flashlight where she meant.

"I see." The enthusiasm was back in his voice.

She knew that despite his protestations of not expecting to find anything, he had gotten caught up in this treasure hunt. She hated to see him disappointed, when it had taken him so long to resume even this tenuous connection to a dream.

"I can't reach that high," he muttered in frustration. "I'll have to get a step stool or something."

He settled on the "or something" of a nearby wooden box. "I can feel it," he said, excitement lacing his voice as he stood on tiptoe...only to tumble off the wobbly box into her arms. They both would have landed on the floor had he not made such a quick recovery. "Are you okay?"

She didn't know how to answer that question. Pressed tightly against him—her hands on the warmth of his cotton T-shirt, her thigh pinned between his denim-clad legs—she was physically unharmed, but desire buzzed through her system like a drug. "We've got to quit meeting like this," she murmured. "The last time we did, we got caught by the police in the park."

"I remember." His golden-gruff voice rolled over her like rich caramel sauce, her favorite flavor.

It would be so easy to stay where she was, to just melt against him, but she tried to be restrained and adult by moving away from him. "I think you'd better use a proper step stool this time."

"That's the first time you've used your librarian voice on me. And you know what? I like it."

She liked his grin and the frequency with which he was flashing it at her lately. When she remembered the grim-faced man who'd first confronted her six weeks ago, she was delighted, encouraged and awed by the change in him.

His leave of absence was almost over now and she wondered how his going back to work would affect him. He never talked about his job.

"You're staring at me," he told her. "What's the matter? Do I have dirt on my face or something?"

"Or something," she murmured softly.

Their eyes met and the now-familiar magic started. She recognized the stages: the anticipation, the sheer pleasure, the appreciation. The bottom line was that she could gaze into his dreamy blue eyes until the sky fell in. And he didn't seem to mind one bit. He didn't look away. Instead, she could see a slow smile starting in his eyes, lighting them with humor while tiny laugh lines crinkled at the far edges.

"You do realize that we still don't know what's in that hidden room." His voice was soft with amusement and something else. Desire maybe? For her?

You're the only one standing here, she told herself. *I don't see any other women in the vicinity.* And while David might love a good treasure hunt, he'd never shown any signs of pursuing it with the same passion that had just been evident in his voice.

That was still no reason for her to stand here like a stagestruck fool.

"The hidden room. Right." She deliberately made her voice brisk. "Let's get back to work."

He got the step stool and resumed his search. "Aha! I found something." Wrapping his fingers around an object, he pulled it forward. "It's a...dusty old bottle of wine."

She could see the disappointment on his face.

"It could still be worth something. I read an article someplace about the value of old wines."

"I doubt that they carried that kind of wine in Chesty's speakeasy. He probably mixed this batch up in the bathtub."

"That was gin, not wine." Carefully taking the bottle from him, she wiped some of the dust and grime from it. "I don't know anything about wines, but this looks like a French label. Come on." She grabbed his hand.

"Where are we going?"

"To my apartment," she replied, dragging him and the dusty bottle of wine up the stairs.

"To do what?"

"Check out the Internet and the World Wide Web."

It wasn't the answer David had hoped for. When he'd held her in his arms a few minutes ago, her warm and responsive body pressed against his, he'd wanted to strip her naked and make love to her, right there against the basement wall.

As she cheerfully bopped up the steps ahead of him, he couldn't help noticing the way the material of her dress clung to her body as lovingly as he'd like to, clinging to the curve of her bottom. He was just

tons on the dress as he'd done once before. This time he worked even faster, and the dress was off her shoulders in a heartbeat. In the meantime, she'd managed to tug his T-shirt over his head before he lowered his mouth to tease the lacy edge of her silky chemise.

Her fingers clung to his bare shoulders as he skillfully moved his hands beneath the material to cup her breast in his palm. The wayward caress provoked an intense pleasure deep within her as he went on to brush his thumb over the rosy peak.

She abandoned reason, and surrendered to the demands of her body, allowing them to dictate her actions as she moved against him. The ensuing friction was a delicious torment.

Her haze of passion was dissipated by a sudden crack followed by David's "Damn!" as he grabbed for his elbow, which he'd hit on the edge of the end table.

Leaping out of the chair and off his lap, she shakenly exclaimed, "What are we doing?"

He groaned. Not now. She wasn't going to call it quits now, was she? He'd die. He wanted her so much it was killing him.

So consumed was he with his thoughts, and his need for her, that it took him a second or two to focus on her next words.

"We should be doing this in the bedroom," she murmured with a sexy smile.

"Amen," he said huskily.

Her bedroom was as colorful as she was, but David wasn't interested in her decorating skills. He was much more fascinated by that incredible little move she made against him when he fluttered his tongue on the roof of her mouth.

The move from the living room wasn't so much an interruption as a building up of anticipation. By the time they were reclining on her bed, Anastasia had undone the zip on his jeans while he'd completely stripped her dress from her.

Fearing that he'd lose control too soon, he deliberately slowed things down, combing his fingers through her hair as he murmured, "Remember that time my grandmother walked in on us?"

"How could I forget?" she huskily replied, kissing his shoulder. "It was only the second time I've blushed all year."

"You said that you had to practice a new finger-play routine. What did you mean by that?"

She frowned at his question. "It's pat-a-cake, itsy-bitsy spider, that sort of thing. Why?"

"Because I got this sexy fantasy about you and finger play. Only it wasn't pat-a-cake, it was more along the lines of this..."

He slipped his fingers to the juncture of her thighs, stealing beneath the silken confines of her panties to the center of her dewy heat, where he practiced his erotic magic on her. He took his time, making sure her pleasure was intense and all-consuming.

"You know how much I enjoy a good treasure hunt," he whispered. "And I can't think of a greater treasure than this..."

When he fastened his lips on her nipple and shifted his fingers in a devilishly erotic move, her back arched and her lips parted in a shivery moan of ecstasy. He felt her climax ripple through her, saw her skin glow and her eyes widen with smoky bliss.

As she lay in a dazed afterglow of satisfaction, David quickly took care of protection and returned to her side. The music in the living room reached a stunning crescendo as she reached for him and guided him home. Feeling the welcome evidence of her continued arousal, his entry was smooth and sure.

When she shifted her hips to take him even deeper, he groaned with blind pleasure. A slave to desire, he moved with primal rhythm, every thrust bringing her closer to fulfillment again. Only when she reached it did he, too, surrender—shouting her name as completion gripped him.

11

"Mmm, that was incredible!" Anastasia murmured with heartfelt satisfaction as she sat in the middle of the rumpled covers on her bed, with David at her side.

"Were you referring to the way we made love or to the bowl of maple pecan ice cream you just devoured?" David inquired dryly.

"Both," she replied before licking the spoon to get the last tantalizing drop of ice cream. Looking over at his mostly full bowl of chocolate-chocolate chip, she said, "Yours is melting."

"I'm working on a new soda-fountain creation, one that wasn't in my grandfather's dog-eared book. But I'll need your help."

"You want me to taste it when you're finished?"

"No, I'll be doing the tasting. I just need you to lie back and get comfortable..." He took the empty bowl from her and set it on the nightstand painted with moons and stars. "That's good," he said as she reclined on the bed. "Now, I call this creation an Anastasia sundae. After unwrapping a fresh Anastasia, and they don't come fresher than you," he added with a wolfish grin as he undid her robe, "you begin with melted ice cream, chocolate-chocolate chip is good." He drizzled it over her bare breasts.

She yelped in surprise. "That's cold!"

"Don't worry. I'll fix that." Lowering his head, he licked the ice cream from her skin, his tongue stroking her with warmth, creating a fire deep within her. The cold liquid had made her nipples tighten, but the heat of his mouth closing around the sensitized peaks was enough to make her back arch off the mattress with bliss.

"Is that a freckle or a chocolate chip?" He formed the words against her, lapping her up. "Mmm, delicious."

Spearing her fingers through his silky black hair, she huskily whispered, "I had no idea you were so creative."

"You bring out the best in me." His voice was rough with passion as he drizzled more ice cream on her. She shivered as the cold liquid hit her skin, and she moaned with pleasure as his mouth and tongue consumed her in a sensual conflagration.

DAVID NEVER KNEW he liked having his big toe licked until he experienced it firsthand the next morning. It took him a second or two to realize that it was Anastasia's cat who was doing the licking.

Startled, he yanked his foot away only to have the cat pounce on it as if it were a mouse. Then he remembered this was the feline who was afraid of mice.

He removed his foot just in the nick of time. His sudden movement spooked the cat, who jumped down after giving him a reproachful look from its blue eyes.

"Sorry," he heard himself whisper as he held out a hand in conciliation. To his surprise, the cat turned around and came back to sniff his fingers and butt her head against his hand in an invitation to pet her.

He'd always liked animals, aside from mice and rats. Growing up, he'd had a dog and a cat both. His grandmother still had a couple of cats, descendants of Hank, the orange tabby that had grown up with him.

He hadn't thought about that cat in years. Since working for the fire department, his thoughts had been consumed with his job. Other than baseball, he had no other interests or hobbies. His identity had been formed by his work.

Lying back against Anastasia's colorful pillows, he figured it was time to take stock of his life. He'd changed since meeting Anastasia and helping his grandmother fulfill her dream. The realization wasn't sudden, it had been creeping up on him for some time. And finding that hidden room last night had reminded him of the pleasure to be had from having a dream, even if the search had only netted him an old bottle of wine.

Dreams made him think of Anastasia. Making love with her had been better than he ever could have dreamed.

"You look deep in thought," she noted sleepily before snuggling close to him to run her bare toes along his leg.

Growling with pleasure, David scooped her half onto his body so that her bare breasts were pressed against his chest. "I was thinking that I should keep the Anastasia sundae as an exclusive recipe for myself."

"I think that's a wise decision," she replied, resting her head atop his heart while swirling her fingers across the flat plain of his abdomen.

Capturing her hand with his, he lifted it to his lips before saying, ''That's the first time you've ever called me wise.''

''Maybe it's the first wise thing you've ever said,'' she retorted, lifting her head to give him a saucy grin and kiss the underside of his jaw.

''What about my suggestion to go with the eggnog ice cream instead of the mince pie for the holidays?'' he asked, nibbling on her fingers. ''That was a wise move, too. We sold out.''

Her smile turned mocking as she said. ''This from a man whose favorite flavor was vanilla when I met him.''

''How did you know my favorite flavor used to be vanilla? I never told you that.''

''I could tell that you were definitely a vanilla kind of guy,'' she said with airy confidence.

''Oh, really?''

''Yes, really. Traditional, stodgy, responsible, bossy, judgmental...''

''Flattery will get you nowhere,'' he mocked.

''You don't need flattery. You have a big enough ego.''

''For a burnt-out arson investigator.''

She frowned at his words which clearly took her by surprise. ''What are you talking about?''

''That's why I was on a leave of absence. To get a better perspective on things.''

She was about to tease him by saying something along the lines of ''Did you boss around your coworkers and aggravate them, too?'' when she saw the somber expression in his blue eyes. He wasn't kidding around. He was serious. "You never told me that."

"Why did you think I was on leave?"

"Claire implied that it was because you wanted to use up all that vacation time you'd accrued."

"That's what I told her."

"Why didn't you say anything before this?"

He shrugged. "What was I supposed to say? That I'm a burnt-out arson investigator? That sounds real appealing."

"I noticed you never talked about your work, which for a workaholic like you should have been a tip-off that something was wrong."

"The old me was a workaholic. But over the past few weeks I've slowly rearranged the priorities in my life."

"So now baseball is number one," she teased.

"No, *you* are." The words came easier than David thought they would. And once he started speaking, he couldn't stop. He went all the way, following his thoughts with customary bluntness. "I love you and I want to marry you."

Her expression was stunned instead of delighted. Without saying a word, she nervously reached for her robe and slipped out of bed.

David could tell this was not a good sign. He might not have asked many women to marry him, but he was pretty sure she was supposed to show some signs of excitement; scream, cry, shout *yes, yes, yes!* Something along those lines.

And okay, sure, Anastasia never did things the regular way, she did them her own way. But even *she* should be doing something other than pacing the floor. Not than he was an expert on the subject of proposals.

"Why do I get the impression that you're not exactly thrilled?" he asked.

"It's just that I never dreamed that you'd propose to me."

Her answer didn't please him. Feeling at a definite disadvantage because he was still naked in her bed while she was rambling around in her robe, he impatiently grabbed for his jeans and yanked them over his hips. "Why not? I'm good enough to sleep with but not to marry?"

"That's not it at all." She gazed at him with dismay in her golden eyes. "I never thought you'd propose to me because you seemed to value your independence as much as I do."

"Are you telling me you don't love me?" he demanded.

"No, I'm not telling you that at all. I *do* love you. I have since you gave that nervous look to the mouse in my car. Well, actually, I was falling in love with you before that, but I knew for sure in the car a few days ago." She shoved her fingers through her tangled long hair before admitting, "The thing is, I don't want a husband telling me what to do. At thirty-three, I've gotten used to doing things my own way."

David couldn't believe her response. "I thought all women wanted to get married."

Now Anastasia turned on him, anger lighting her eyes. "That's a stupid thing to say!"

"No more stupid than you saying you don't want a husband telling you what to do."

"I wasn't stupid for saying that," she replied, "but I was an idiot for thinking you'd ever understand how I feel!"

"I'LL TELL YOU what's stupid!" Hattie shouted from the corner floor lamp, despite the fact that they couldn't hear her. "That I did all this work to get them together, to have David propose, and she says no! I can't believe this! We all gather here in time to hear the marriage proposal, and this happens."

"We didn't take this possibility into consideration," Muriel admitted.

Hattie glared at her. "No kidding."

"We focused on getting David to realize how much he loved Anastasia and on her learning how much she loved him," Betty added. "Who knew Anastasia would need convincing about marriage as well as love?"

The rhetorical question didn't sit well with Hattie. "You're the oldest, it's your job to know these things."

"Hey, this is *your* assignment," Betty snapped. "I already dealt with Jason and Heather. Anastasia is your baby."

"If she was my baby I'd put her over my knee and spank her."

"Yeah, right," Muriel scoffed. "This from a fairy godmother who can't hurt a flea."

"But she loves him," Hattie wailed. "She said so."

"We should have guessed that she'd be nervous about sharing her life, about marriage. She's so gun-shy about losing her autonomy. She's got such a zest for life that others have tried to quell. All that attitude she has was bound to create a few problems." Muriel spoke with great authority.

Hattie was not impressed. In fact, she was becoming increasingly agitated by the second as she circled the rim of the reflecting bowl atop the torchier floor lamp. Her lavender hat, the same one she'd worn to Jason's wedding, had become dislodged by the emphatic shaking of her head as she kept muttering "No, this can't be happening." The wringing of her hands was turning the magic wand in her fingers a glowing red until, like a flame shooter, it released a sudden burst of blazing energy.

"Fire!" everyone in the bedroom, human and fairy godmother, all shouted at once.

12

ONE MINUTE she was arguing with David, and the next, the bedroom was filled with smoke. Anastasia had noticed a small puff of fire, like a miniature volcano going off in the far corner of the room, before her eyes started watering from the strange purple-tinted billowing clouds of smoke.

"We've got to get out of here," David said, grabbing hold of her and guiding her toward the front door. "Where's your fire extinguisher?"

"Here, under the kitchen sink."

Snatching it up, he raced back to the bedroom. Her heart was in her throat until she heard the whoosh of the fire extinguisher a moment later and then David calling out, "It's okay. You don't have to call the fire department. It must have been a short in your floor lamp. Created a lot of smoke, but didn't do much harm otherwise. We caught it in time."

"Thank heavens." Those few seconds when he'd been on his own in her smoke-filled bedroom had seemed like an eternity. She stood in the bedroom doorway, almost afraid to see what damage had been done. Surprisingly, there wasn't much.

"It's the strangest fire I've ever seen, though." David was studying the surrounding area. "For all that smoke, there are no burn marks aside from the top of this lamp. This dresser is right next to the lamp but there isn't a mark on it. And the minute I opened your bedroom window once I was sure the fire was out, the smoke just flew out of here like a bat out of hell.''

''Maybe the ceiling fan helped move the smoke out,'' she said.

''It wasn't turned on.'' David shook his head. ''It's almost like something out of one of those stories you tell the kids, where someone waved a magic wand or something and, presto, the smoke was gone.''

''NICE GOING!'' Betty said, glaring at a sooty Hattie clinging to the edge of the bed's painted headboard.

''I didn't do it on purpose,'' she wailed, shoving the blackened rim of her hat out of her eyes. ''It was an accident. I was upset.''

''And you think we weren't? But you don't see us starting a fire, now, do you?'' Betty's voice reflected her anger.

''How could I know that hand wringing would start a fire?'' Hattie said, clutching her slightly fried magic wand in one hand. ''You should have told me.''

''Don't try and put this on me,'' Betty retorted. ''Look what you did to my T-shirt.'' She held it away from her body, pointing to the black marks across the What Are You Looking At? lettering.

''I'll fix it,'' Hattie hurriedly offered. A wave of her wand replaced the T-shirt with a new one, in pastel lilac this time. Seeing the furious look on Betty's face, she quickly waved her wand again and returned the shirt to its white color.

But Betty showed no signs of being appeased. "If you think that makes everything all right, you're sadly mistaken."

"At least my magic wand still works," Hattie noted, hugging it to her gratefully.

"For all the good that does us." Betty put both hands on her ample hips to glare at her youngest sibling with blatant disapproval. "I'm telling you, I may be lenient about some things, but this really takes the cake."

Hattie glared right back, holding her hat's drooping rim out of her eyes to do so. "You were the one who said this case would be a piece of cake."

"Quiet, you two," Muriel ordered them. "Anastasia and David are talking."

"I'VE GOTTA TELL YOU, this isn't the way I imagined my morning would be going," David said as he set the fire extinguisher back on the floor. "I mean, I've heard of things getting hot in the bedroom, but this is ridiculous."

"You've got that right," Anastasia agreed with a nervous laugh. Her hands were shaking from the adrenaline still racing through her system, so she stuck them in the pocket of her blue chenille robe, where she found a catnip toy. "Xena! Have you seen Xena?" she asked, her voice frantic.

David nodded. "I saw her in the living room, diving under that weird-looking table."

Anastasia raced into the living room, going down on her knees to peer under the table. Xena's blue eyes blinked back at her reproachfully. "Sorry about that,"

Anastasia murmured. "I know how you hate catastrophes. I do, too. In fact, I feel faint."

"Probably because all the blood rushes to your brain when you have your fanny in the air like that. Not that it isn't a sexy fanny, don't get me wrong," David said as he hunkered down beside her. "Here, sit up." He gently straightened her, propping her up as she swayed a bit. Her back rested against his chest as he went on to say, "I've got to tell you that this marriage proposal isn't exactly going the way I'd hoped it would. Not that I have much experience with this sort of thing. Fires, sure, those I can handle. I can figure out burn patterns, sort out clues from charred debris on a fire site. But I can't seem to figure *you* out."

"I've been accused of being complicated," Anastasia admitted in a small voice. She felt cherished, cradled in his arms.

"I can understand why."

"Not that you're any simple idiot yourself," she hurriedly assured him.

"I'll take that as a compliment...I think."

"You know what I mean," she replied, loving the way his golden-gruff voice reverberated through her as he spoke.

"The scary thing is that yeah, I *do* know what you mean. I may not always be able to figure you out, but over the past few weeks I've learned to know *what* you mean even if I don't know *why* you mean it." Resting his chin on the crown of her head, he said, "Before we were interrupted by me putting my foot in my mouth and the ensuing fire, you said you valued your independence and thought I did, too. Well, you were right. I do value my independence. Trust me when I say that I don't go running around proposing to women after making love to them.''

"That's reassuring," she said tartly, sitting up straighter as the idea of him with someone else speared her with jealousy.

He grinned. "Your fiery nature is one of the things I love about you," he told her.

She eyed him suspiciously. "Guys have told me that before, only to try and change me into a demure little thing.''

"I don't think even one of those fairy godmothers you're so fond of drawing would be able to change you into a demure little thing," he noted dryly. "It ain't gonna happen.''

"That's for sure.''

"See, we agree on that." Combing his fingers through her long hair, he murmured, "I'm sorry to have to tell you this, but my grandmother will not approve of me living in sin with you. She may come after you with a shotgun or a vintage ice-cream scoop and demand that you make an honest man of me. I just felt it fair to warn you, for your own safety.''

It took her a second to realize that instead of being bossy or angry, he was actually teasing her.

"So you only asked me to marry you because you were afraid of my being assaulted by your grandmother wielding an ice-cream scoop, is that it?" she asked, going along with him.

"Pretty much, yeah," he said with a slow smile that lit his dreamy blue eyes and made her knees weak. "Given a choice, I'd be happy to make wild passionate love with you and forget the conventions, but there is my grandmother to consider. And while it's true that she once told me that she had no plans to marry, that she'd just live with a guy because she's on social security, I don't have that excuse to fall back on."

"Not for a few years yet anyway," she agreed, realizing that he was making all this up to try and put her at ease. She'd never loved him more than she did at that moment.

And that's when Anastasia realized that being married to David didn't have to mean giving up who she is.

"Gee, you sure know how to make a guy feel good…"

Taking a deep breath, she interrupted him to say, "Yes."

"And modest about it, too."

"No, I mean yes, I want to marry you!"

He eyed her uncertainly. "Was that a yes or a no?"

Turning in his arms to face him, she said, "It was and is a yes."

"Took you long enough," he muttered before taking her into his arms and kissing her. He pulled away a second later. "Wait, I just realized I messed up."

"Felt like you were doing just fine to me," she whispered seductively.

"I meant about my proposal of marriage. I didn't tell you what I decided about going back to work. All I did was tell you that when I met you I was a burnt-out arson investigator. That's not the case anymore. I can now remember what I liked in the beginning about the job—looking for clues as if I were on a treasure hunt. It's recharged my commitment to my work.''

"You were a workaholic. It never sounded as if you weren't committed to your work. If anything, perhaps you were overcommitted to it.''

"That was before I had you to distract me.''

"Are you saying you think I'm a distraction?''

"You're the best possible distraction.'' Taking her hand, he said, "Come on.''

"Where are we going?'' Anastasia looked at him in confusion. "The bedroom is the other way.''

"To get that bottle of wine I found. I think we should toast our engagement.'' When they reached the kitchen, he searched out the dusty bottle.

"Wait!'' She grabbed it from his hands. "Before we break open the wine, let me check my e-mail to see if anyone has answered the notes I sent last night.''

"It's just an old bottle of fermented grape juice,'' he said as he followed her to the living room, where she reached for and powered up her laptop.

"Mmm,'' she murmured absently as she accessed her new e-mail. "Holy cow!''

"You sound like Harry Caray from Wrigley Field,'' David noted in amusement.

"That old bottle of fermented grape juice, as you called it, happens to be worth fifty thousand dollars, give or take a buck or two.''

He laughed at her words. "Yeah, right. Very funny.''

"I'm not kidding," she assured him. "Take a look for yourself. I got several e-mails about the wine, which is a rare French vintage. Two bona fide wine dealers e-mailed me with firm offers to buy it for fifty thousand dollars."

David was so stunned, the bottle almost slipped from his fingers. He and Anastasia both made a diving grab and saved it. Setting it safety on the end table, they stared at it in awe.

"It looks like Chesty did have some hidden treasure, after all," she whispered.

A knock on the front door interrupted them. It was Claire, looking perky and pretty in khaki slacks and a Big Dipper polo shirt. "I was looking for David, he wasn't in his apartment, ah, there you are," she said as if there was nothing unusual in finding her grandson bare-chested in Anastasia's apartment. "I went down to the basement and found this strange open door to a little storage area built into the corner. Did you find the treasure you were looking for?"

David shrugged and deliberately kept his voice low-key. "We found a bottle of wine."

"Oh." Claire's voice reflected her disappointment.

"Worth fifty thousand dollars," he added with a grin.

Putting one hand to her chest, she gasped. "Oh, my stars!"

"The money is yours," David told her.

"Nonsense. You found the hidden room and the wine. The money is yours."

"No way. It was in your building. It belongs to you."

"Maybe you both could split it," Anastasia interrupted them to suggest.

"Excellent idea," Claire said. "I told you from the beginning, David, that Anastasia was a smart woman."

"I never doubted that for a minute," David replied.

Claire frowned at Anastasia with a reproachful look. "But she may not be smart enough to know what's good for her where matrimony is concerned."

"Before you come after me with an ice-cream scoop, I plan on making an honest man of your grandson and marrying him," Anastasia assured her friend with a teasing grin.

"He's always been an honest man," Claire said proudly, tears gathering in her eyes, "but you'll make him a *happy* one."

"I told you I'd teach him how to have fun," Anastasia said with a sassy smile, "and I never go back on a promise."

"I'm counting on that," David murmured as he took her in his arms.

Epilogue

One year later

"THE RESPONSIBILITY is tremendous," Muriel stated solemnly, her voice echoing in the soaring confines of the church.

"I agree." Betty nodded, tugging on the hem of her "No Whining" T-shirt.

"Does this hat go with this dress?" Hattie fussed with her turquoise ensemble, smoothing the elaborate ruffles on her dress and tugging on the dyed-to-match gloves before leaning over the church-balcony railing to ask, "Shouldn't they be starting the wedding by now?"

"Hold on to your horses," Betty said.

"You don't mean that literally, do you?" Hattie asked, magic wand at the ready should she need to conjure up a pair of horses.

Betty hurriedly shook her head. "It's just a phrase, for petunia's sake. Don't go creating any scenes. That hat you're wearing is dramatic enough."

Hattie preened. So did the white dove on her elaborate chapeau. "I'm so glad you like it."

"It's so you," Betty drawled.

"Thank you, but I'm so nervous I can't stand still." Batting her wings faster than a hummingbird, she flew upward with such speed that she bumped into the head of a gilded angel hanging high on the church wall. "Oh dear, I hit the angel again."

"I think it's a reflection of your latent hostility toward guardian angels caused by your gilded-wing envy," Muriel stated, a recently acquired pair of reading glasses perched on her nose, making her look like Sigmund Freud on steroids.

"Oh, horsefeathers!" Hattie scoffed. "It's just that I'm anxious for the ceremony to begin."

"I'm with you," Betty agreed. "Who would have thought that Anastasia would be the most conservative of all the Knight triplets and want a year-long engagement followed by a big formal wedding in the church where she was christened?"

"It all started here," Hattie noted with a sentimental sniff. Floating back to the balcony, she dabbed at her teary eyes with a lacy handkerchief.

Betty's booming voice was reflective as she said, "Who knew that the noisy crying Knight triplets would turn out so well?"

"Wasn't it our job to know that?" Hattie asked with a frown.

Betty shook her head. "No, it was our job to unite them with their soul mates and we've done that."

"Anastasia and David aren't married yet," Muriel cautioned.

"How can you be so calm?" Heather demanded as Anastasia lounged in the bridal waiting area of the church. "When I was about to marry Jason I was a nervous wreck."

"And so you should have been," Anastasia said with a grin. "My brother had a reputation. Not only was he bossy as all get out, but he held the dubious title of Chicago's Sexiest Bachelor. Until you snagged him."

"He snagged me, actually," Heather replied. "Or maybe we snagged each other."

"You look so gorgeous in that wedding dress, Anastasia, I almost wish I hadn't eloped." Courtney entered the conversation for the first time.

"I kept telling David I was going to get married in red velvet overalls and a hot-pink top along with my neon orange shoes or my combat boots. He still doesn't know about this dress. You really think it looks okay?" She checked the mirror one more time. The white wedding dress, with its bare shoulders and open neckline, featured a bodice of heavy beaded lace with a dropped waist leading to a rich satin skirt with a romantic train that trailed behind her. Her hair was piled on top of her head, where a veil cascaded from the tip of her crown down her back in frothy abandon.

"It's gorgeous and so are you."

Claire, her matron of honor, joined them with a status report. "The guests are all here. It's almost time to start."

"How's Ira holding up?"

"He keeps saying he's never been a best man before, but I keep telling him he's the best man for me," Claire replied with loving affection.

Anastasia was so pleased that Claire had found happiness with Ira. "Who'd have thought that he and David would get along so well? Or that David would have my two brothers as his groomsmen. I'm still questioning the wisdom of that move," Anastasia said with a shake of her head. "I wouldn't put it past them to try and talk him out of marrying me."

"IT'S STILL not too late," Jason was telling David in another anteroom in the church. "You could still make a run for it."

"We'd cover for you," Ryan added. "We could say you were abducted by aliens."

"Like that alien stripper you had at my bachelor party last night?" David inquired.

"Hey, she was a fan of the 'X-Files'."

"I told you I didn't want a stripper." David straightened his bow tie. He'd never worn a tux before and now he knew why. But Anastasia had insisted on his wearing formal attire. He just prayed she didn't pull a prank and show up in something outlandish. Actually, he just prayed she showed up. He knew she was in the church already. Her dad had stopped by to tell him that much, but had refused to reveal what she was wearing.

"We thought you were kidding when you told us no stripper," Ryan said, looking no more comfortable in a tux than David did. Jason and Ira were the only ones who looked totally at ease in the formal wear.

"You do realize that because you two got me a stripper for my party, my friends hired a male stripper for Anastasia's party yesterday." Seeing the way his soon-to-be brothers-in-laws' jaws dropped, David had to smile. "Ah, you two look a little surprised."

"They didn't!" Jason and Ryan said in unison.

"They sure did. And what's more, Anastasia took great pleasure in telling me every single detail about the guy dressed as a big bad cop who took it all off. Or just about all."

Jason and Ryan shuddered.

"You two should know better than to aggravate your sister," their dad said. "Let that be a lesson to you."

"Yeah," Ryan noted wryly. "The lesson is to never let Anastasia, Heather and Courtney get together in the same room without male supervision."

"They're together right now," David observed.

"Yes, but your grandmother is with them," Jason replied.

"For all the good it will do," David retorted.

"What do you mean?" Ira demanded, joining the conversation for the first time.

"My grandmother is the one who actually booked the male stripper," David said.

"YOU GIRLS DECENT in there?" Ira asked from outside the door. "David's got a present for his bride."

"He can't see her until she walks down the aisle," Claire said through the paneled door, before opening it a crack. "He's not out there with you, is he?"

"No. He asked me to give this to her. You look lovely, Claire," he added, bowing gallantly as she opened the door. "You too, Anastasia," he added as she scooted past Claire to see what Ira had brought from David.

"Don't tell him what she's wearing. She wants to surprise him," Claire told Ira.

"My lips are sealed. I must say, that Victorian garnet and pearl necklace that David chose from my shop looks exceptional with that dress."

Meanwhile, Anastasia was eagerly ripping off the elegant foil paper on the package. Heather and Courtney hung over her shoulder, curious to see what David had gotten her. "Jewelry. I bet it's more jewelry," Heather said.

"It's a kid's book." Courtney's voice reflected her confusion.

David had written inside the cover:

For My Frog Princess,

I fell in love with you the first time I heard you reading this story to the kids. Reddit. Thought it was time you had your own copy so we could love happily ever after. You made me believe that sometimes dreams do come true.

Your husband-to-be,
David

"You're crying over a kid's book," Heather said in astonishment.

"It's not just any kid's book. It's *The Frog Princess,* one of my favorites. This strange-looking frog turns out to be a lovely young woman who is…"

"A princess," Heather and Courtney said in unison.

"No, a librarian." Hugging the book to her bosom, she wiped the tears away before turning to Ira with a brilliant smile.

"Tell David I love him and I think we should get this show on the road and get married."

"IT'S STILL NOT TOO LATE to play Dean Martin's 'Everybody Loves Somebody'," her father whispered as he took her by the arm in preparation for walking down the aisle.

"Forget it," she whispered back. "Don't you have any words of advice for me, Daddy?"

"You haven't called me that since you were twelve," he said gruffly. "As for words of advice, you don't need them. You're a smart cookie, but just remember that underneath it all you'll still always be my little girl. Uh-oh, there's our cue."

As she walked down the aisle on the arm of her father, Anastasia was filled with a wonderful sense of rightness. She'd been afraid that after years of avoiding matrimony she might experience some panic at the last minute. But her request for a year-long engagement, during which she and David had lived together, had convinced her deep down that he was the man for her—the special soul mate who truly understood her. And on those rare occasions when he didn't, he was willing to listen while she translated for him.

He was waiting for her at the altar, looking sexy as could be in a dark tux. She saw his gorgeous blue eyes widen with appreciation at his first sight of her in her wedding gown. She could feel his love for her as she walked closer to him. And then she was there, by his side, her hand in his.

The actual ceremony passed in a blur until the minister said, "Do you, Anastasia, take this man, David, to be your lawful husband, to love and honor and cherish him from this day forward?"

There was a brief pause as everyone in the church held their breath.

Leaning forward over the balcony railing, all three fairy godmothers yelled at the top of their lungs, *"She does! She does!"*

Turning her head, Anastasia gazed back at the otherwise-empty choir balcony, almost as if she could hear them.

Then, with a flash of her sassy grin, she faced the minister, the same one she'd inadvertently punched in the nose at her christening as a baby, before turning to David and saying, "I do. *Soitenly,* I do!"

"SHE SAW US," Hattie murmured in awe.

"Or heard us," Muriel said. "Or thought she did."

Betty tried to unobtrusively wipe her eyes with the sleeve of her long-sleeved T-shirt before shooting her sisters a warning glance. "These are tears of relief, in case you're wondering."

"Well, these are tears of joy." Hattie didn't even bother to wipe them away with her handkerchief. "I'm so glad that we've finally accomplished our mission with the Knight triplets. All three of them are with their soul mates now."

After blowing her nose loudly enough to do a fog-horn proud, Betty resumed her position of authority. "Yes, well, there's just one thing I have to say to you two."

"What's that?" Hattie asked nervously.

"Damn, but we're good!" Betty rewarded her two sisters with a high-five slap in their hands. "Let the celebrations begin!"

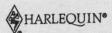 

Take 2 bestselling love stories FREE

Plus get a FREE surprise gift!

**WHEN THINGS START TO HEAT UP
HIRE A BODYGUARD...**

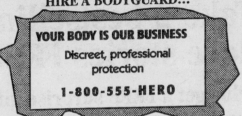

YOUR BODY IS OUR BUSINESS

Discreet, professional
protection

1-800-555-HERO

AND THEN IT GETS HOTTER!

There's a bodyguard agency in San Francisco where you can always find a HERO FOR HIRE, and the man of your sexiest fantasies.... Five of your favorite Temptation authors have just been there:

JOANN ROSS *1-800-HERO*
August 1998
KATE HOFFMANN *A BODY TO DIE FOR*
September 1998
PATRICIA RYAN *IN HOT PURSUIT*
October 1998
MARGARET BROWNLEY *BODY LANGUAGE*
November 1998
RUTH JEAN DALE *A PRIVATE EYEFUL*
December 1998

HERO FOR HIRE
A blockbuster miniseries.

Available at your favorite retail outlet.